DOG'S LIFE

DOG'S LIFE

James Rogers

JONATHAN CAPE
THIRTY-TWO BEDFORD SQUARE LONDON

First published 1986
Copyright © 1986 by James Rogers
Jonathan Cape Ltd, 32 Bedford Square, London WC1B 3EL

British Library Cataloguing in Publication Data
Rogers, James
Dog's Life.
I. Title
823'.914[F]   PR6068.03/
ISBN 0 224 02360 8

Phototypeset by Computape (Pickering) Ltd, North Yorkshire
Printed in Great Britain by
Ebenezer Baylis and Son Ltd
The Trinity Press, Worcester and London

For Ann, my mother

Contents

PART ONE

1	Watching	11
2	Pin-up Girls	18
3	The Carving Knife	25
4	Alice Gets the Labour	34
5	Private Worlds	45
6	Love	51
7	Cross-purposes	58
8	Medicine Cabinet	65
9	Looking after Animals	73
10	Window-breaking	80
11	Tenth Anniversary	83

PART TWO

12	Angus Is Angry	97
13	Dog's Life	102
14	The Better Future	108
15	King Brown	114
16	The Prodigy	123
17	Norman the Cyberman	129
18	Norman Unbound	136
19	At the Bee Colony	140
20	Breakfast	147
21	Observations	152

22	Further Observations	157
23	The Head of Science	161
24	Hospital	167
25	Justin Sells the Mice	173
	Appendage	181

PART ONE

I

Watching

I am in the garden. I am eight years old.

My mother and father, Alice and Ken, are seated in the floral-pattern garden chairs on the patio. The french windows are open, the sound of the new stereogram in the lounge coming in insipid, easy-listening washes. I look through the disinfectant-smelling leaves of the small pine tree and see Alice, blown-up, seven months pregnant in her maternity smock. The leaves faintly scour my soft cheeks. Ken and Alice are having an argument, as often happens at this hour of the day. It has been the trend over the last few months that these early evening arguments (always with drinks on the patio) have become more ferocious than once was usual. They are, of course, completely unaware that I am listening to them.

This was before Ken's promotion, only a few weeks before. He was a salesman; he went out in the car every morning, a silvery-blue Ford Cortina, his company car. After the promotion he did much the same and was paid a nominally greater sum for doing so. It was, none the less, a promotion. Alice had an old Vauxhall for doing the shopping and 'collecting the kids'. That was Angus my brother, aged five, who had just started at school and was not doing at all well, and me. I was excellent at school.

Last winter I was watching the clouds that my breath formed, sitting in the front seat of Ken's car. I undid the glove compartment to look at the things Ken kept in there: a repair manual, an Ordnance Survey map of London and the Home Counties, and a pair of driving gloves with a small pink stain like that of lipstick on them. Everything very much as you would expect it. He was peeling sheets of the *Daily Express* off the windscreen, brittle and splintering in the frost. The car was outside because there was only one garage and Alice's car was kept in there. Ken sometimes mumbled something about having a double garage built on so that both cars could go in it, and maybe he'd extend the lounge through into the old garage. I could imagine Alice neatly labelling the two bays of the double garage — with initials like our four toothbrushes.

Ken turned the key in the ignition; it clicked and was followed by the asthmatic dog's wheeze. He tried a few more times. Angus and I were walking over the crunching frost towards the blue garage door. Ken didn't want to have to take the Vauxhall: an old car doesn't make a good impression on the customers. I am waiting for his usual complaint on occasions like this. It comes: 'They don't make them like they used to.' Cars. The frost is tingling under my feet.

We are driving past the frozen duck-pond on the way to school. Angus is sitting in the back and says, 'Why are you so fat?' Then he gurgles his salivating baby's laughter. He is extraordinarily stupid and vulgar. Because I make no attempt to hit Angus, Ken is impressed by my self-control and maturity. Angus knows full well that I will not hit him while our father is there. He knows I will push him into the hawthorn bush inside the school gate. Ken is grumbling to himself about the car.

I say, 'What's wrong with your car, Daddy?' He explains, predictably enough, that he must have used too much choke and flooded the engine.

'Do you know what flooding the engine means?' Ken likes to take a constructive part in our education, especially as regards matters boys should know about.

'It is when the carburettor floods with petrol.' I knew this from before: exactly the same thing happened last March.

We are turning into the road where the school is. I can see the other children walking along the pavement through a hole where the frost has melted on the window. Ken says, 'Mummy will ring Mrs Richards and get her to collect you. Remember, won't you? And go straight to her car with Andrew. Don't go running around in the road, it's easy to slip on the black ice.' I am picking up my satchel from the floor: there is no carpet like there is in the Cortina. That wouldn't impress the customers. 'You won't forget, will you? And keep an eye on Angus. He's not used to the roads yet.'

'Of course. Goodbye, Daddy!'

The door slams shut.

Of course I won't forget: I never forget anything. I'll even watch for the black ice, if that is what you wish.

Mrs Richards is Andrew's mother. At first acquaintance, when I was three, I rather liked her. There was something exciting about her, a slight sense of the glamorous – even something faintly sinful. She was an improvement, at any rate, on anaemic Alice. And Mrs Richards – Mavis – liked me because she thought I was much more intelligent than the other children. Like most people she liked you if you took the trouble to talk to her and so express an interest in her. She thought I was *trustworthy* because I talked to her. I would go out to the kitchen while she was preparing food and talk to her about gardening, things that had happened in the newspapers, and show-jumping, a great interest of hers. She was particularly fond of me as from the day I said, 'You should be a show-jumper on the television, Mrs Richards. You're very good at riding.' She laughed in such a way as to say really how nice of me, but it wasn't true. Secretly, I knew, she was delighted.

People love being flattered. I had learnt this young: no matter how far-fetched the compliment they love being flattered. To demonstrate what I mean by this: on another occasion she was sunbathing in the garden by their new swimming pool (the only one in their road), wearing a small, orange bikini. It was the day after a beauty contest had been broadcast on the television and I said she was prettier than Miss World. She laughed and snorted, 'Honestly! You little devil! What would your father say?' But, of course, she would not so much as mention it. She was secretly ecstatic. It was our little secret. I found it interesting how easily people can have misconceptions about their bodies. Mavis's was flabby and wrinkled with folds of fat under her arms that the bikini straps dug into. There were calluses of hard skin on her feet. In the bathroom cabinet she kept a whole range of Dr Scholl chiropody products.

Angus was walking by my side across the frost, beginning to plot his escape from the hawthorn bush. I was wondering if we would go round to Mavis's house after school, and whether Alice would walk round to collect us. Mavis and Alice are great friends. Andrew will want to play football: we'll put Angus in goal between the herbaceous border and the wheelbarrow, and kick the ball at him as hard as possible. The ball will go over the swimming pool and, with luck, up into the paddock. We will then force him to go and get it. He is terrified of the horse. Mavis will say Andrew has to go in and change if he's going to play football. I'll follow her into the kitchen and talk to her.

'Is that a new food-mixer, Mrs Richards?'

'Yes, that's right. How observant you are.' I will think, yes, in contrast to your moronic son I certainly must seem observant. 'It's very nice.' She loves compliments on her possessions. Everyone does. She loves it when I say 'You've been to the hairdresser', when she comes back looking like a slightly worn Lucille Ball.

Her daughter Christine will get home from school at a quarter past four. She goes to the grammar school in the town on the school bus. She is thirteen. Everyone says, 'What a pretty girl Christine is becoming.' There, for once, they are right. She has a beautiful smile. At the weekends she sometimes wears her mini-skirt, or her blue bikini when she is by the new pool. Once, going up the stairs to use the bathroom, I looked into her bedroom. It was a little shrine where she pinned her Pony Club rosettes on the wall, and laid out her cosmetics and porcelain horses on top of the chest of drawers. I could smell her smells in the room. Personal, secretive, dreamy smells.

The old Vauxhall was turning round at the far end of the road. Angus was walking in front of me, planning his quick dash past the hawthorn bush. Stephen Walker was throwing a Superbounce ball to Daniel Porter – one of a particularly unpleasant brood of children – who was running cautiously, leaving flattened pads in the glistening frost. He fell over and cried out. Caroline Briggs, the democratically elected head-girl (the headmaster was a socialist of sorts, a fact which bothered Ken), was walking behind us. Well, if I can't push Angus into the bush I'll save it up for later. He knows that: he knows that I never forget anything. I keep perfect score. And, of course, he is wrong: I am not fat. It's just the only thing he can think of. In some sense he must say it because he wants to be punished. He laughs his spluttering, croaking happiness when he knows that I am about to take punitive measures. Some people are like that: they like being made to suffer. He disgusts me, like all children.

We lived off the main road in the 'mock Tudor' house with the sloping drive and Alice's rose garden. In the spring Alice was pregnant *again*. Before it was showing, before that thing like a shiny bladder swelled out from her pallid torso, she came into the room where Angus and I were playing and said, 'Children, you're going to have a little brother or sister. Mummy is pregnant *again*.' What was that strange intonation on the last word, I wondered? Were we supposed to be impressed? Always Alice had enjoyed those cryptic turns of phrase which she felt kept everyone guessing about her; musing over the strange mysteries of her chemistry and her illnesses, her enigmatic sighs and pauses.

I had heard her talking to Mavis: she said, 'I'm pregnant again, you know.' This time it was with a weary, resigned-to-the-world, what-*could*-one-*do*? intonation. As if the kettle were broken, *again*. She was showing Mavis an arrangement of her dried flowers and berries. Making these was her hobby.

Mavis said, 'Isn't that beautiful! You're so clever at things like this. I'm going to get the secret out of you one of these days!' Alice smiled her enigmatic smile. It was rather like making the baby – everyone would wonder how you'd managed it. She was holding a piece of the green foam-rubber stuff, dry and brittle like the honeycomb in a Crunchie, into which she poked the stalks of the flowers, in holes she had gouged with a certain air of sadistic pleasure with a pipe-cleaner. She would then cut the stiff foam with the breadknife so that it would fit into the urn she was using. She had made so many of these arrangements that the 'guest bedroom' was filled with them. It smelt of a dull, ossified autumn smell, and of plastic: the green honeycomb. It made me feel sick. But apparently – this was one of the things Ken and Alice were arguing about on the patio – the 'new arrival' was going to change all this. The baby in Alice's tummy.

Alice wanted a girl this time. I remembered Mavis and her over housewives' coffee.
 Mavis said, 'It would be nice to have a girl, wouldn't it?'
 Alice agreed: boys were nice, but two was plenty. She smiled at me, to say it was just a joke really.
 'Don't tease him!' Mavis said, laughing her corncrake's laugh and also smiling.
 I smiled back at her. It was one of their jokes – what a 'handful' little boys were. But they agreed – I had listened in many times on this particular discussion – it was very important not to joke too much about this: children can be awfully sensitive. They don't always understand that you're just having a joke.
 Still smiling hard at Mavis I said, 'What will you call the baby if it's a little girl, Mummy?'
 'Oh, I haven't really thought about that yet, sweetie,' Alice said.
 'You could call it Mavis after Mrs Richards.'
 Mavis hooted. 'Oh no! It's a terrible name. I'm sure the poor little thing wouldn't want to be called Mavis.'
 Of course not; I had known that. This was something else designed to please Mavis, by way of being an indirect compliment. Like the food-mixer it was a sort of possession of hers, her name. It worked: she was smiling lovingly at me, thinking what a nice and clever little boy I was.

I was sitting behind the pine tree, the largest of the row of ten, and thus the one which afforded the best cover. Alice was saying how we'd *have* to move into a bigger house, there wasn't room for another child here. Paul's room was too small to put Angus in there too: she didn't like bunk-beds; you couldn't not have a guest bedroom. What did Ken know about running a house? A house with bigger rooms, or five bedrooms. Ken wanted to know what bloody guests, and anyway what was wrong with the couch in his 'study'? The floral-pattern chair creaked as he got up to pour himself another drink. 'We can't *afford* to move, yet,' he said.

Ken and Alice were always arguing about what they could or could not afford. The word seemed to occur in their every conversation. The mortgage, the rise, next year, sales figures, the promotion: this was the vocabulary with which this argument was conducted. No, we couldn't afford Spain this year. We would go to the Broads again, or Devon. Ken would wear his captain's hat as he solemnly navigated us through the waterways of the Broads. Alice would make the tea and complain about how long the gas took. She would comment on the coots and moorhens she'd seen. They would argue about the difference. 'You know nothing!' Ken would say. Alice would remind him that *she* had a botany O level pass.

Sitting silently behind my pine tree I watched Ken sluice Johnnie Walker over the ice in a tumbler he got free at a petrol station. The ice comes out of a pineapple-shaped ice bucket. Ken stays standing at the bar. 'It'll have to wait,' he says in a final spurt of rage, 'and you could start by clearing all that bloody rubbish out of the spare room.' With noble resignation Alice ignores this. Will Ken say 'Excuse my French', his usual appendage to such words? I think not: he is too intent upon registering the gravity of his feeling on the subject. They will not speak for the rest of the evening, other than in cursory, dutiful attempts to assure the children that nothing is wrong. The day will end and they will climb into bed having brushed their teeth with the initialled toothbrushes. They'll kiss good night and Alice will take a couple of Disprin for her perennial headache. Ken might belch and murmur a half-apology. Alice will fall asleep feeling like a martyr.

Perhaps tomorrow I will go round to Mavis's and swim in the pool. Perhaps Christine will be there.

2

Pin-up Girls

A few weeks later I was on holiday from school and Ken said he would take me along to work with him one day. I could meet some of his business colleagues, perhaps even learn a bit. 'You can't start learning too young,' I heard him say to Alice, who thought perhaps wouldn't I rather stay and help her do the gardening, as she could hardly bend over now, she was so inflated with the baby? Was Ken getting a little spiteful gratification from this, I wondered? Were we two men together, and Alice could stay and suffer the gardening?

We drove through Surrey villages, a special route Ken had worked out for himself that avoided a right-hand turn on to the London road, until the green belt gave way to miles of straggling suburbs where new offices and 1930s terraces glared at each other like dogs disputing territory. We were the men going out hunting to bring home the bacon. Alice was at home, tending the crops with the infants being put to help. Angus would be given the task of weeding a flower bed: 'That's right, sweetie, but pull those nasty docks right up by the roots or they take hold again.' Angus would be dribbling, singing 'Happy Birthday to You', a song he had sung every day for the last week even though it had been no one's birthday.

Ken had no conception of doing anything useful and purposeful that was not business. He knew that there were other people with other activities, but they were different, somehow alien to him and his world. There were working-class people:

they worked in factories to make the things that business men sold and bought. They belonged to Trade Unions, organisations upon which Ken would discourse with some vehemence after a few whiskies. Working-class people were, for the most part, 'decent enough people', but they were unalterably different and played no part in the crucial, important matter of the world, which was business. He did not 'think' these things, just as one does not think about eating, sleeping and breathing. They were sort of vital assumptions upon which his organism depended.

And there was another class of other people, that vague, amorphous category into which Ken's brain fitted everything like people he saw on television, landed gentry and artists. While not actually his betters, these people filled a superior slot in the world by dint of its vagarious nature. Their existence was summed up in his favoured expression, 'Well, I don't understand that sort of thing.' He thought of them as people who read difficult Sunday newspapers.

What Ken did understand was that if you worked hard in business you got on. Scroungers and layabouts did not get on. Ken's world was a neat, ordered meritocracy where everyone, in the end, got their just deserts. It was not always fair – 'Don't expect everything to be fair, the world isn't a fair place' – but Ken enjoyed a fundamental assumption that there was in the world of business some kind of final come-uppance for those who strayed from his ill-defined code of conduct. Without this nourishing thought his world would have collapsed and the gaping horror of futility would have stared him in the face.

We drove over the Thames and Ken pointed down at a long thin rowing boat scudding over the black water. 'They're probably training for the boat race,' he said. 'I want you to get a good education.' He liked short, sharp statements like that. Immediate no-nonsense jumps from one thought to another. I agreed with him: I nodded and concentrated with a serious expression on the handle of the glove compartment as if thinking long and hard about my future, about education and business, the matters of the world. Ken said, '*You* can do it, you know.'

I didn't doubt it for a moment. I came top in every subject at school without even trying. Daniel Porter came to me and begged me to do his arithmetic for him. Like a good business man I did so, at a price.

We were in the dark grey corridor of a modern building that seemed as if still only half-built. Ken pushed open a door and I walked through into the shabby, makeshift office that smelt of photocopying. 'Dave,' Ken said, taking the man's hand and shaking it with a confident grasp, 'Paul, my eldest boy. Taking him out for the day.'

Dave, a smaller man with thin, straw-coloured hair seemed delighted to see me. 'Well, hello young man. Learning to follow in your dad's footsteps, eh? Jolly good.' He was chummy, ingratiating. 'Right, here we are, let's sit you down here, young fellow-me-lad, and your dad and me will discuss some business.' The teeth he flashed at me were yellow, the enamel lacerated with fine cracks like the glaze on a very old plate.

'Sheila will get you a glass of milk,' he said, signalling with his head to the secretary. She stood up from the typewriter where she worked and walked towards the door we had come in by. 'And how about something to keep you amused?' He had gone to a table in the corner that was messily piled with magazines and papers like a doctor's waiting-room. 'Think this'll fit the bill!' He laughed his bouncing chuckle and raised his short arm to Ken's shoulder to motion him through into the office. The first door that Sheila had gone through finally clicked shut. It was painted with orange undercoat. Dave turned back from his door and said, 'Now, young man, do you think I can entrust you with a very important piece of business?' His wit clearly amused him.

I replied in the assertive no-nonsense manner Ken favoured, 'Yes.'

'Excellent! You can ask Sheila – Miss Hibbard – to bring two cups of coffee through. Right we are.' The door slipped shut and then I heard their muffled, serious, business voices, occasionally embroidered with the big laugh from Dave's small body.

I picked up the copies of *Motor Magazine* and *Motor Cycle Weekly* that Dave had placed for me on the low table at the side of Sheila's desk. I swivelled round in the office chair, lifting my feet off the scrobiculated, oakum-like carpet so that the seat spun freely for five revolutions. In the corner next to the magazine table was an old, curving wood hatstand hung with coats, jackets and a black shoulder bag I took to be Sheila's. There were more coats than could possibly belong to Sheila and Dave, so I guessed this to be a sort of cloakroom for the other people who worked here; perhaps for travelling salesmen like Ken. Pinned on the wall behind it was a topless woman with sun-tanned skin and dark, curling hair, kneeling at the edge of the sea and grinning ecstatically. From a conch she was pouring water down herself, the water forming a small rivulet between her breasts and glistening on the gold chain belt that hung around her stomach, above a white bikini bottom. Her nipples were dark and pointed, about the size of the drawing pins. In actuality they would be much larger, the width of gingernuts.

This was a man's room, not Sheila's room. She was a kind of appendage to it. It was rather like going to the barber's with Alice. I recalled with glee the occasion on which I had pointed at the packets of Durex and asked Alice in a loud voice what they were. I had known perfectly well. I was five at that time.

On the television once I heard the phrase 'The way to a man's heart is through his stomach'. It was a commercial for food, for small balls of meat in a pale, creamy sauce dotted with slivers of mushroom. The wife stood behind her husband with arms folded over the front of her apron, smiling happily, not unlike the topless girl with the conch and gold belt, as her husband raised the fork to his mouth, savoured the food a moment with an interrogatory facial expression, smacked his lips, and said, 'How *do* you do it darling?' She winked knowingly at the camera as if in conspiracy and the surge of music came up. She knew *the secret*.

This was the way to a man's heart. At least, it was one way to a man's heart. There were others. Kneeling topless in the spumy sea, for example; that seemed a way. And another, that Dave fancied he had the knack of: making extravagant shows of friendship towards a man's children. Thus was Dave so chummy to me. People, I decided, are nice to each other when they want something.

Sheila came back with a glass of pink, frothing milkshake. She put it on the table and smiled her wide, gregarious smile at me. 'There you are, Paul,' she said. She had big brown eyes with long, curving eyelashes dark with mascara, and possibly false. A wave of powerful perfume followed her around, generating an aura I envisaged as being like that of radioactive people in films. It was a smell that said: *Sex*. She had returned to her desk and was about to switch on the dictaphone from which she typed her letters.

'Miss Hibbard,' I said, 'Mr Packman said would you make two cups of coffee.' I had read his name on the door: adults prefer it if children politely use their surnames, then they can say 'Call me Jim!' or 'You can call me Samantha if you'd like', in a friendly way that says how much they like you.

'Thank you, Paul,' Sheila said. 'You can call me Sheila if you like.' She had got up to put the kettle on. The surge of sex-smelling perfume passed and she rubbed the top of my head with her hand, patted me, much as you would a dog you liked.

'Would you like me to help?' I said, standing and following her towards the sugar-encrusted table.

'That's awfully sweet of you.' Smiling.

Unscrewing the cap of the Nescafé I toyed with the idea of saying something outrageous to her, something that would shatter her illusions about my being a nice, considerate, well-mannered little boy. 'Can I put my hand up your skirt?' or 'I would like to sniff your bum'. I visualised her face. I tossed the idea around my brain, savouring the probable ramifications. She would not dare tell Dave, not at least until we had gone, because it would not be good for business to tell Ken that his son had made improper suggestions to the secretary.

But I liked Sheila, and her euphoric wash of cheap perfume.

Ken was proud of me: I was outstanding at school, took a healthy interest in sports and athletics, was well-mannered, able in conversation with adults, never childish. My last school report had said: 'Paul is an extremely able boy who works hard.' 'Shows keen interest. An outgoing and very intelligent boy. Consistently produces good work. Well done!'

I was a model pupil, what every teacher and parent craved. I was coveted, loved, envied, revered, desired and cherished.

When the school inspector came to our school it was my desk

to which Mr Burton brought him. The inspector commented on my excellent handwriting and asked me what my project was about. Mr Burton stood back, his arms folded like the housewife serving the meatballs. I was his mushroom sauce, his perfect crenellations of carrot and translucent garden peas. His secret. He stood well back behind the inspector. In the sheen of the newly painted door I could almost see his expansive, well-fed-animal grin; proud, smug and happy.

'It's on Isambard Kingdom Brunel, sir. This is a picture of the *Great Western* that he designed in 1833. It sailed from Bristol to New York, the first ship to make regular crossings of the Atlantic. The following illustration is of his next ship, the *Great Britain*, the first large ship to be constructed of iron and to have a screw propeller.' I recited this without reference to written text, looking up into the face of the inspector. Mr Burton simmered with a quiet ecstasy.

'Do you have aspirations towards being a civil engineer yourself, Paul?' the inspector inquired.

'It is one career that I have given some consideration to, sir.'

'Jolly good.' He was almost perturbed by my precocity. Mirages of instant promotion gleamed in Mr Burton's mind's eye.

Alice was proud of me too. Alice showed me off to her friends; to Mavis, to ladies from the Women's Institute, to fellow guests at Tupperware parties and the annual cocktail party at Mavis's when the children were allowed to stay up. Christine would be there too. Alice paraded me and I walked round with my neatly parted hair, smiling at the guests as I offered them cheese-and-pineapple snacks on cocktail sticks pronged into a halved melon, or petite, glazed sausage rolls Mavis made.

'What a well-behaved boy!' they said.

'What have you been learning about at school?'

'The Kings and Queens of England.'

'I bet you can't name them all!' Hoots of laughter over their pink gins and Martinis.

In fact I could. I could name every monarch since Egbert in 827. Sometimes I would impress this awesome reserve of knowledge upon them. When I reached Ethelred in 865 one would invariably, almost in obligation to some unwritten law, say, 'Ethelred the Unready!' Then, unremonstratingly, I would explain that Ethelred the Unready was actually the second Ethelred (978–1016), son of King Edgar, succeeding to the throne after the murder of his half-brother Edward the Martyr. I would then ask if they cared for a cheese pastry or a stuffed olive.

I never forget anything.

3

The Carving Knife

When I was younger, two, three, four, Alice would shout at me for hours at a time. There was never a whiplash of uncontrollable rage, just a constant, repetitive tip-tap, redolent of the Chinese water torture I had read so enthusiastically about in *A Shorter History of Torture*. Generally she was preoccupied with something else, scrubbing or peeling the potatoes, dusting, trimming the edges of the lawn with a giant pair of scissors, or making her dried flower arrangements. I would be in another room, drawing aeroplanes in my bedroom, wheeling a red fire engine over the sitting-room carpet, looking at the way my penis shrivelled in the cold water of the paddling pool.

'Paul . . . ! Paul . . . ! Porl . . . !' as regular as clockwork, with odd, disinterested changes of intonation, and occasionally, at the slightest stimulation – a little ruction of sound from my quarter or the suggestion of a movement – there would be an up-tempo emphasis, a change in the rate of repetition, a snappy, barking-dachshund sound: 'Paul!'

It went back into the mists of time, to the pushchair, to the vast, soft woolly pram with the hollow click-clock of the coloured balls and the rustling straw of my bunny rabbit's innards. It receded back into the swamp of my first perceptions, part of a vague, ghostly world, an endless twilight. Like rain that has crept up, and imperceptibly is tapping its fragile fingers on the window-panes, it had no beginning. It was the beginning of time itself; the endless, ambient soundtrack of my babyhood.

It was so one summer afternoon a few months before Angus was born. I was three. I was in the garden plucking the dried husks of daffodil stalks from a flowerbed and erecting them into wigwams on the lawn. Alice was in the kitchen, puffed up like a fungus, bulging through her yellow maternity smock, slicing fine slivers of lime for a dessert she was making, slotting the end-pieces into her mouth and chewing them with a tight-eyed, pained pleasure. It was Christine who had told me that pregnant women sometimes crave to eat odd things on some mysterious demand for vitamins or minerals from the body growing within them. She said when Mavis was pregnant with Andrew she ate chocolates and tinned sardines while she was hiding in the bathroom. Christine said you could smell the fish if you went in there after she came out.

Alice was droning 'Paul!' every ten seconds or so. 'Will you stop doing that!' if she looked out through the kitchen door and saw me standing on the flowerbed. 'Stop that immediately!' if there was a tangible, immediate threat to her fragrant herb garden. This was about the time of my first experiments with her, gauging and carefully tabulating in my memory the intensity of reaction that a specific action would induce. There were many variables though, so the same action had to be performed at each hour of the day, and when she was engaged in different pursuits. For example, if she was flower-arranging at three in the afternoon, at the dining table, and I banged two of my toy cars together and made a child's car-crashing sound followed by an *uhuh uhuh* of police car siren, she would react with a quieter 'Stop doing that!' than if she was eating, talking to Mavis, dusting, or polishing the brass. She was generally quieter in the afternoons, so long as it wasn't too hot or, conversely, hadn't rained on the washing. The excrescence of her pregnancy was, however, at this time, another factor that tended to produce data fluctuations.

Sometimes I trotted over to the kitchen door and stared up at her with my bad-dog look, and temporarily she was appeased, said, 'Well, don't do it again', and patted my hair or kissed my cheek, though she didn't like having to bend with the bellyful of Angus prohibiting her freedom of movement. Certainly by the time he was born I had full mastery in controlling the vicissitudes of her temper. I was capable of keeping her at an even keel of anger, never getting to the point of wanting to spank me, but never feeling completely relaxed. Simmering, I called it. If I did anything more serious than trample on the herb garden it merited not only the sad-dog gaze, but an immediate declaration of apology *before* she had time to start screaming at me. I would go straight up to her, look her in the eye, and say in the no-nonsense business manner, 'I'm sorry, Mummy, it won't happen again.' It never failed. She was too weak – too sentimental. She was someone who would never hurt an animal.

It was the afternoon of Christine's seventh birthday, and I was invited to her party. Like all 7-year-olds she did not want silly, screaming 3-year-olds at *her* party, but I would see to it that she did not see me in that light. I would impress her with my serious, perceptive dialogue, my wit and sophistication.

Alice called out from the kitchen that it was time to go. As the last experiment in this afternoon's schedule I pretended not to have heard. Seven seconds elapsed.

'Porl!' – louder, more piercing. I relished this easy power, a power so binding on Alice's sensitivity that I believe I could have induced a miscarriage had I been so minded, and saved myself the existence of Angus. I left the tepees of daffodil stalks on the lawn and cantered gaily to wash my hands with the pungent bar of Camay. With neatly parted hair and no dirt under my fingernails I came down the stairs and took up my present for Christine. We walked out of the front door, up the steep, sun-dappled Tarmac of the drive, and along the pavement under the elm trees, my hand held up and cupped in hers. How sweet we must have looked! The mother and son, just like any other, just like the mothers and children you see walking down summer sunny avenues all the time, happy and peaceful.

'You won't misbehave, will you?' she asked. 'I don't want you being influenced by Justin Burrows and his sort.'

'No, of course not, Mummy.' Pause. 'I think he's immature.'

Alice was always delighted when I repeated what I had heard her saying. I could have repeated verbatim the entire of her last harangue against Justin and his 'unpleasant family', but that would have unnerved her: it was better carefully to recombine odd parts of her pronouncements, so as to give them the tang of original, freshly considered perceptions. This is what is commonly called intelligence.

We arrived. Alice ferried me through the hall, thick with coats and duffel-bags and discarded roller-skates, into the lounge where the dining table had been pulled out from the wall and covered with a huge, old tablecloth, one it was clearly acceptable for the children to muck up. It was bedecked with sandwiches of egg and cress, and cheese and chutney; with tiny, wizened sausages on cocktail sticks; different coloured jellies with bananas and smartie-men; dainty Chinese bowls Mavis had got on offer; and fluffy yellow and turquoise cakes. In the centre of the table an expectant gap where the birthday cake would be laid at the appropriate time. Most of the children had arrived and were in the garden, through the open french windows. Mrs Dickinson was passing the last few things through the small hatchway that opened out from the kitchen. It was through this tiny door that I smilingly passed plates to Mavis when I went for tea. Mrs Dickinson was placing two big jugs of orange and lemon squash, jingling with cubes of ice, in the hatch. Mavis took them to the table. Dressed in marigold slacks and a fern-green blouse, she turned round to the table of infant offal.

'Hello Paul!' she said. 'Why don't you go and join the other kids in the garden. We'll be ready in a mo. Is that a present you've got there? How kind of you.'

I put the present down with the others on the coffee table, exchanged one or two pleasantries with Mavis, and walked through into the garden. Norman Edwards, clearly put up to it by his companion, Timothy Torkinghorn, was throwing clods of earth at the Wendy house. Inside, behind the closed windows, Jacqueline Reynolds and Denise Clark cowered behind their outspread hands. A cloud of earth struck the glass and dissolved into a fine, dusty spray.

'You'll bust the windows!' Timothy howled as Norman threw another clod of earth. It was clear that the usual routine of persecuting Norman was well under way. The earth careered past the Wendy house and struck one of Mavis's foxgloves. Its radiant mauve head drooped apathetically as the stalk snapped and tilted drunkenly towards the lawn.

'Now you've done it!'
'Norman's broken the flower!'
'Norman did it!'

Within seconds I was witnessing baying, ululating Red Indian noises and football terrace chants of nor mun nor mun nor mun! Even at this age I had already developed a sharp sense of distrust and loathing for the pack instinct that would so readily manifest itself in my peers, as indeed in my elders. The way everyone would crowd like hyenas around the weakest. The way none of them would dare act independently of the mass.

'All right! Stop all this nonsense at once. Everyone in!' Mavis had emerged. For the first time I caught a brief glimpse of Christine; she was standing by the construction of bricks referred to as the barbecue. She was wearing a new dress, white with pink and peppermint stripes. Mavis was still shouting, 'Be quiet! No, I don't care if Norman broke the flower. I'm sure it was an accident. Come on.'

'Wasn't wasn't wasn't!' the crowd of children howled at her. Mavis was shouting to try and bring order to the chanting, laughing and gurgling children. Squeaks, howls, croaking parodistic chortles and motor car noises joined together in a blanket of sound as the children crowded round her feet and moved like one vibrant cell-culture through into the lounge. I saw Christine standing back from the pack of her so-called friends looking aloof and dignified. I felt that there was someone who perceived this spectacle as I did.

'Hello,' she said. She looked miserable.

'Happy Birthday,' I said, and she smiled and said thank you. I noticed her little white pop-socks: they were new too.

There was a green and white Dansette record player in the corner of the room playing songs: 'Here We Go Round The Mulberry Bush' and 'Bobby Shaftoe', sung in a quaint, rustic accent with an old church hall piano accompaniment, echoey and slightly discordant. It was for the kids: chummy, patronising, sick-making. We were playing Musical Chairs, everyone throwing themselves around the room, screaming and struggling like drowning kittens when Mavis lifted off the gramophone needle with a wrenching scrape. Christine, I could see, thought it horrible. But it was her party so she had to pretend to be having fun. I kicked a chair from underneath Andrew so that he bruised his head, then dropped out of the game by disdainfully refusing to find a chair.

'Paul's out!' Andrew shouted. I memorised the transgression: he would be punished. I felt contempt for the delight he took in this game.

After Musical Chairs there was another game. We all queued to be blindfolded by Mrs Dickinson, then walked sightlessly to a dart-board and attempted to place a tag as near the bull's-eye as possible. Justin Burrows tried to look through the blindfold and Mrs Dickinson disqualified him. 'You dishonest boy! Everyone else is playing for the sport of it and you have to go and cheat. You ought to be ashamed of yourself!' Mrs Dickinson, like Alice and Mavis, did not like Justin. He was a bad sort, and it was only politeness that induced Mavis to invite him to Christine's party.

I could not accept her thesis – that everyone was playing for the sport of it. There was a two shilling prize and glory besides. I had taken the precaution before the game of working out that the bull's eye was exactly at the height of my lower lip: so I won the two shillings by a more sophisticated method of cheating. Everyone said how clever I was and Mavis stroked my neatly parted hair.

Mavis bore the yellow cake with seven candles in white, buttercup-fashioned holders (like golf-tees) through to the table. Justin was trying to jab a cocktail stick, disgorged of its shrivelled chipolata, into Norman's eye. 'Stop that! You foul little urchin!' Mavis screamed at him. 'Haven't you caused enough trouble for one day?' Then she surprised everyone. She stared at him for a moment, then, in a fit of pique, swung her free arm round and slapped the side of his head. He swayed under the impact of the blow but showed no sign of pain. He sat dead still in the chair in the moment of silence that fell over the room. His cheek went from its rosy, plum hue to a big, blazing swell of purple, and his eyes watered and flared. He stood up and charged past Mavis like a small bull, seizing the knife from the frilly silver-foiled cake base in her hand. The cake plummeted from Mavis's hand and broke up, littered with speckles of flame, over the wooden-tiled floor. The dog,

Bananas, lurched from under the table and thrust his snout into the cake, then howled as Mavis tripped on his tail and stabbed her heel into his paw. Above the rising crescendo of the children I heard a quick 'Fucking dog' slip out before it could be restrained. Mrs Dickinson was running towards the kitchen door, but Justin had already barricaded it with one of Mavis's stainless steel kitchen stools. One with a blue and yellow plastic wicker-pattern seat.

I resolved to move to the best vantage point from which to view the ensuing action.

'Stop this immediately!' Mrs Dickinson shouted. It reminded me of Alice: did mothers take lessons in phrases to use with children? Was there a section in Dr Spock? She shouldered the kitchen door. 'Come along. Come out this instant!'

All the children were crowding towards the kitchen hatch to view the caged animal. I looked at Mavis's face, stained with her smeared coral-pink lipstick and splatters of the spilt orange squash. Christine looked as though she were going to cry. Mavis hammered her palm down on the table top, the remnants of jelly quivered in sympathy, and everyone was silent.

'Everybody sit down,' she said with as much authority as she could muster. There was only the banging of chair legs and susurration of quickly drawn breaths. 'Now, everyone is going to keep perfectly calm.' It was as though she were assuming a part in a film about a sinking ship. Then there was a fine tinkling, strangely hollow in sound, from the kitchen.

'Justin's broken it!' Norman blurted out and Mavis stared hatefully at him. His ears flared bright red. Mavis walked calmly to the hatch.

'Now, Justin . . . ' she began, gentle but firm.

With equal calm, in an unwavering, emotionless voice, he interjected, 'I'm going to kill myself.'

'Now, let's not be silly over some – ' Mavis was nearly knocked over by the surge of tiny rodent-like bodies that piled up around her legs. She started screaming. From where I stood, behind everyone, up on the coffee table, I could see Justin perfectly and the knife poised tremulously over his sleeveless wrist. Mrs Dickinson was once again seating the children.

Mavis said, 'Justin, don't play with the knife. It could be very dangerous. Now, what say you put it down and come back out and we'll say no more about the whole thing? How's that?' She was doing everything she could to smile understandingly at him.

'Why?' He peered malignantly into her eyes. 'I'll be dead in two minutes, so what's the point?' There was a fearful logic to it. Denise let out a strange, withering scream. She was white.

'It's all right. Everyone stay where you are. Justin's just being a bit silly.'

'Dead in two minutes,' he repeated like a mantra.

'Justin, you never know what might – '

'Dead in two minutes.' The tone was triumphal, inevitable. The blade teasingly caressed the white skin and its crazy-paving of thin blue veins.

Mavis panicked. 'Bloody well stop that!'

'Two minutes.'

Denise was ghost-white. I watched as she toppled forward on to the table. Everyone's gaze remained fixed on the bizarre, dangerous spectacle in the hatch. 'Now, I'm coming in,' Mavis said, and stood on a chair so she could clamber up into the hatch.

'Dead.' His eyes stared coldly, remorselessly, relishing the fear he had instilled in Mavis. Timothy Torkinghorn pointed at Mavis's knickers and giggled. I saw Christine, kneeling and picking up the clumps of her shattered cake and the jagged sheets of yellow icing. Mavis's girth now filled the hatch, her stockinged legs flailing behind as she climbed through. The children stared at her rump, as if the hatch were a TV screen that had gone off but that everyone still gazed at for want of anything better to do with their eyes.

'Come on,' Mrs Dickinson said, 'let's all help clear up the mess.' Mrs Dickinson was in charge of the Cub Scouts, a job which gave her the privilege of appending the name of some animal or other to her own: wolf, bear or something. She was now assuming her Scout-mistress role; rallying the troops. Justin's voice was still there, repeating 'Two minutes', but she seemed to have defused the situation. The children were ferreting round on the floor picking up pieces of cake and sausage roll. Bananas the spaniel had sneaked back in from the garden where he had gone to nurse his damaged paw, and was running round wagging his tail and licking the children's faces. He liked this new game where everyone seemed to be pretending to be a dog. I remained where I was though, waiting. Mavis was putting her knees on to the Formica worktop, thus opening the space in the hatch that enabled me to see Justin again. He remained motionless.

Mavis screamed. She was scrambling over the Formica. The children were rushing again at the hatch.

I saw the vivid streak of blood opening up like the ripped skin of overripe fruit. Justin's steely eyes peered at the arm that he held up for inspection, the knife still clenched firm in his fist. He appeared as if in a trance. He held the arm still as the first spurt of blood ran down the palm and dribbled over on to the white, 'marble-effect' tiles. Mrs Dickinson was holding her hand over her mouth. All the children were silent. Mavis grabbed Justin by the shoulders and he looked up into her face with an expression of nonchalant disinterest. She shouted out, 'Ambulance!' It sounded like a strangled croak.

'Garden. Now. Everyone,' Mrs Dickinson said, and for once she was obeyed instantly. I watched as Mavis wrapped a tea-towel around Justin's wrist. As Mrs Dickinson hurriedly dialled nines on the telephone, I took a last look at the flaring red mushroom patterns forming on the tea-towel, and caught Justin's eye. He was beginning to look frightened. I went out into the garden.

4

Alice Gets the Labour

Rachel, my sister, was born a month prematurely.

Ken was up north on business, selling his machines, when Alice went into labour. She was at the garden table with a bucket of soapy water and a kitchen brush, cleaning the garden gnomes. 'They do get *so* dirty,' she would say. She hated dirtiness in the garden. Andrew and I were in the patch of rough grass at the top of the garden, before the fence and the trees, looking for a snake to bury in the sand-pit where Angus played.

Andrew said, 'What would your mum do?' I gave this some consideration. Every time Ken had sworn at her over the last couple of months she had threatened him with a miscarriage; the doctor had told her how sensitive she was, which piece of information had given her seemingly endless cause for delight. It seemed logical that the premature death of Angus in the sand-pit might actually induce the oft-vaunted miscarriage. I was picturing her awful mourning of Angus, her doughy eyes and the way the little blue veins on her temples would stand up and throb and, worst of all, the threnodial whine she would be sure to employ.

Then she emitted a long, painful howl and stumbled back from the table where the gnomes – Arthur, Benjamin, Rupert, Lance and Sailor – smiled their benign and implacable grins at her. There was no sign of Angus, no sound. I was momentarily shocked by the possibility that I was possessed of some psychokinetic power that had instantly brought to fruition the contemplated course of events. Alice moaned. 'It's coming!' as though in the grip of a ferocious devil, then started taking small pigeon-steps across the lawn, her toes pointing inwards, her breathing a hideous, gulping noise. There was still no sign of Angus.

'She's having her baby,' Andrew suddenly realised.

'I am perfectly well aware of that, thank you.'

Christine had told me another good story, some time before, about a woman who went to the lavatory thinking she wanted to shit (Christine giggled when she used that word) and her baby had started coming out. I was imagining Alice spread-eagled on the bathroom mat.

There was a loud ringing noise as Alice dropped the telephone. 'We've got to help!' Andrew pleaded, but I restrained him.

'Do you mind not interfering with my experiment?'

I was particularly interested to see how Alice would cope with this novel situation. Not well, it seemed: she let out another howl and then started gasping the word 'Ambulance' into the receiver of the phone. I had always found her undignified when under stress. I supposed this to be part of her desired image of being 'sensitive'. Her face was wobbling and tears were dribbling down it. Andrew was growing more impatient to go and help her.

'There's nothing whatsoever we can do,' I reminded him, 'this thing we must let take its course.'

Now she started calling out, 'Paul! Please, Paul . . . Angus!' Andrew was on his feet before I could stop him. 'Give it time,' I told him, 'the experiment isn't concluded yet.' He stared at me incredulously, fear transforming his face. 'There's no room for sentimentality in science.'

'But she's calling you.'

'Be quiet.'

I took note. As I had suspected for some time now, for Andrew science was just another child's make-believe. A game. He was no use.

Angus had appeared. He was leaning out of the bathroom window singing 'Happy Birthday to You'. Alice struggled out on to the patio and called up to him, 'Angus, find your brother, find Paul!' She was quite hysterical.

'Maa mee may kee funee noise,' he replied.

'Please! Please be a good boy! *Find Paul!*' Angus stayed where he was, looking confused, the sun glinting off a dribble of saliva on his chin. 'Go – And – Find – Paul!' she mouthed as though talking to someone who was deaf. 'Please! Be a good boy now. PLEASE!' She had broken. She was collapsing on the patio, moaning.

It was me she needed now Ken was away. I was the protector and provider.

Andrew tried to move and I pinned him down with the stick that I had inserted a three-inch nail in. 'She is *my* mother. This is my experiment. You are dismissed as from the termination of this experiment.' Alice moaned as though she were being sick.

'Poooorl!'

Her voice was altered by the tears and mucus that filled her nose. She was fumbling with the phone again. 'Oh please please please!' she shouted into the silent receiver. 'Please please please,' until the word became no more than an incomprehensible noise that would have meant nothing even if someone had answered.

In truth there was something I could have done: I had lied to Andrew. I could have reconnected the telephone. You see, it was quite common practice: whenever I was going to leave Alice on her own for a while, when I might be at any distance from the house, I normally unplugged it so as to keep a firmer rein on her activities. She was for ever moaning to Ken that the telephone wasn't working and on two occasions had called out a man from the Post Office. Mechanical things she regarded as exclusively a man's job, so she complained endlessly to Ken about how it always worked when the man from the Post Office came, but then the next day she'd try and ring Mavis and it was completely dead. I don't know how many arguments between the two of them were sparked off by this point. I, of course, was meticulous about plugging it back in before Ken or the GPO man arrived; and she was either too stupid – or too timid about mechanical things as her mother had taught her to be – ever to think of looking at the connection box. Oh, and as a safeguard – just in case she ever did look – I always left a selection of Angus's toy cars on the carpet by the plug, thus automatically implicating him. 'Angus was playing around again. Naughty Angus.'

None the less, it was done now.

Alice was talking *to* the telephone. I took note: talking to inanimate objects, as she did with the gnomes. She was pleading with it to work; crying all over it.

Angus had come down. 'Angus, please. Go into the woods and call out to Paul. It's very urgent. Mummy's poorly, very poorly.'

'Paul-ee,' he echoed, 'very paul-ee.'

'Go on!' He began to walk down into the garden, past the row of Christmas trees, ten of them ascending in size like Christine's set of Russian nesting dolls; one planted every January since Ken and Alice had lived in the house. Alice used to say how much they reminded her of Christmas, which was nice. Which was funny because she did little else all Christmas but complain about how overworked she was, how difficult it was getting the turkey and all the bits ready.

'Paul! Paul-ee,' Angus burbled. The sound mixed strangely with a distant groan from Alice. I began a countdown: *five*. Alice was again trying to get life out of the phone and Andrew was trying to get my attention. *Four*. She was tapping the receiver of the phone on the carpet! *Three*. Angus arrived at the edge of the long grass and called my name again. The one thing he did not want to do was to go into the grass, because I had told him stories about there being a pit of cobras in it. *Two*. Alice might be regretting now that she had so long affected feminine ineptitude with mechanical things: now, when it really mattered. *One*. If nothing else I had taught her a lesson. Angus looked as though he'd seen a tarantula.

I stood up and ran down through the grass calling 'Mummy'. Angus looked intensely relieved to see me. When I reached the french windows, breathing fast as though I had run miles to save her, Alice couldn't express her love for me strongly enough. 'Paul! Please. I'm so glad you're here. Mummy's having her baby, the phone won't work, please . . . '

'All right. Stay calm, Mummy. You mustn't worry about anything.' I tried the phone and she started burbling that it wasn't working, she was sure, she'd tried and tried. 'Sounds like it's been disconnected,' I said.

'It's always going wrong. I've told your father, I don't know . . . '

'Look! It's been unplugged down here. How could that have happened?' Her eyes had followed me. There was no need to spell it out. Even in her deranged condition she would take in the pile of toy cars. And I had long since grown out of toy cars, just in case there was any confusion. Angus stood on the patio gawping aimlessly at the house.

'Angus,' she said, 'oh, why can't he be good and clever like you, I don't know.' It all comes out under pressure, you see.

When I had reconnected the phone and rung for the ambulance I went upstairs and fetched a damp face flannel for Alice to dab her face with. It was like oil of cloves after the drill. 'How proud your father will be,' she said. I then phoned Mavis and explained the situation. It was all arranged: Angus and I would stay with her while Alice was in hospital. Alice said how sweet I was.

I am in Mavis's kitchen. She is rolling pastry on the Formica worktop, sprinkling flour that stains her brown fingers and their talon-like nails. I am sitting at the 'breakfast bar', a narrow, cupboardless stretch of the worktop where the yellow and blue plastic wicker chairs stand. There are to be at least three days spent in Mavis's house: three days under the same roof as Christine, sharing meals with her, using the same bathroom and the swinging bench in the garden ('the swinging sixties!' Mavis jokes) and, of course, the new swimming pool. There is one problem: the presence of Andrew and Angus. I will have to deal with that.

'Your mum will be out of hospital before you know it,' Mavis says. 'It's not like the old days when they used to keep you in for an age. Do you remember when Mummy was having Angus? I bet you do, you're very clever. Not like me. Brain like a sieve. You see when you get to my age!'

'You're not very old, Mrs Richards.' Mavis hoots with laughter.

'Of course, I can remember things that happened twenty years ago as if it was yesterday and I couldn't even tell you what I did this morning. Sometimes I walk into a room and I've forgotten why I went in there!' She laughs again.

At around this time there was an advertising stunt for a brand of motor oil, tyres, or fluffy leopardskin seat cover. This promotion used a mythological creature called 'the groundhog' – it must have been tyres: they clung to the ground – that people festooned all over their cars. I used to wonder even then why it was people were so happy to do this. The groundhog had a long trumpet-like snout that was always to remind me of Mavis, and the characteristic laugh she referred to as 'hooting'.

'Why don't you pop down and have a swim with Andy and Angus? I'm sure I must be boring you! Don't mind me, I'll just carry on. I remember once I was talking to Harry and he'd left the house and gone . . . ' Predictably enough this was Mavis's story about the time Harry drove the whole way into town and back and she'd been in the kitchen talking through the hatch to him the whole time. 'Have I told you before? You should stop me. I'm always repeating myself.'

'You mentioned it once, I think. It is funny, isn't it?' You see how charming I was.

'Well, why don't you go and have that swim now? Best not to swim after you've eaten, you'll get stomach cramps.'

Mavis was a mine of information on people who had drowned as a result of stomach cramps. She would regale me with stories of drownings, people burning in fires caused by electrical faults, people being struck by lightning. She would interrupt herself at intervals with, 'Really! I shouldn't be telling you this. Look at poor old Angus, he's gone quite white.'

'He has a naturally pale complexion,' I would reassure her.

It was a world stricken with arbitrary natural disasters; littered with death, with scandal, with psychopaths and child-molesters, though of course that was one thing she managed to desist from telling me about. It was a world where nowhere, and no one, was safe. Where anything could happen. It was the world of Mavis's newspapers. None of these things ever *happened* in her immediate proximity, and I doubt she really thought they might. But they were things that could have happened to someone at Harry's office, things that had happened to someone whose brother they met on holiday last year in Majorca. This was the way Mavis embroidered the fabric of her dull life. Occasionally remembering the suitable protestations of horror, outrage or sympathy, she would delightedly and animatedly talk for hours on these things. I used to wonder if one day something truly awful might not happen to her.

She was laying the slice of floury pastry over the pie dish and pressing round the edges with a round-bladed knife. She no longer had the knife Justin had putatively tried to kill himself with; she had thrown it away, not wanting to be reminded. It was interesting, I reflected, how that incident, the one thing of genuine newspaper proportions that had actually happened to her, was so well buried, and absolutely never spoken of. She scratched at her red, sunburnt skin, leaving marks from the flour on her chest, above the plump opening of her cleavage.

'Now, I've got to go and water the garden. You go and have that swim with the boys.' As she said this she put the floury hands around my chest, beneath my arms, as if to lift me. I smiled at her, then we walked out into the hall. Out of the kitchen it was easier to detect her aroma, a faintly musky, rodent-like smell, tinged with the slight suggestion of unwashed towel or stale soap. I felt that it was somehow a secretive smell, a private smell. To my young mind it evoked sex, the unventilated rooms where I imagined people having sex. I thought of Sheila, and her smell, and the wave of perfume.

Mavis liked to touch me: it had become a kind of ritual between us.

I was what is termed an 'early developer'. By this, the summer of my yet-to-be-completed ninth year, the yearnings of the sexual life had already taken a strong grip on me. As in the other facets of my life I was accelerated to an almost unnatural degree.

I watched Christine sunning herself on the yellow Lilo that rocked on the swelling, undulating surface of the glittering water. I think at first she was quite unaware of my long, caressing appraisals of her body, thinking, perhaps, that I was too young to be interested in that sort of thing. She was desperately wrong. She dozed or read her book, *Brave New World* by Aldous Huxley, occasionally resting it on the soft puppy fat of her tummy and dipping her hands into the water to paddle the Lilo back into the light of the descending sun. As the afternoons waned the sun sank behind the horse chestnut trees that divided the paddock and the field from the pool and the garden, and her body would be dappled with the enchanting, flickering patterns of the shadows. Sometimes her neck would bend slowly, cautiously up, her hand raise the black science fiction sun-glasses from her eyes, and she would look at me with her inquisitive, kindly schoolteacher's frown and say, 'You all right sitting there? Aren't you bored?'

I was never bored, never.

'Oh well,' she'd say in her lyrical, whimsical voice, and pull the sun-glasses back over her twinkling blue eyes. A wasp buzzed round her head and she flapped her paperback at it. Then she might put the book down again and reach for the small make-up bag she always carried on her deserted raft. She would look in the mirror as she traced two fine, bold crescents of glossy red lipstick on to her quaintly pursed lips. Sometimes as she turned the tiny mirror the sunlight flashed off it into my eyes.

'Paul,' she said, 'be a sweetie and fetch me a drink. I'll get wet if I move and my oil will wash off.' That was the sun-tan lotion she covered her svelte body with. I walked to the house to fetch Coke or bitter lemon made with Mavis's Soda Font Soft Drinks Maker. I brought the glass out with two straws and jingling ice cubes and reached over the edge of the pool to hand it to her. She smiled at me, the wrinkles at the sides of her mouth forming, the dimples deepening at the canthi of her lips.

Where were Andrew and Angus throughout this idyll? Why were they not ruining it by running round the pool, dive-bombing, making whizzing noises, splashing screaming squawking in their hideous, brash children's voices? Why weren't they playing water polo with Andrew's FA regulation football signed by Geoff Hurst? Or chortling and braying over the infantile humour of Andrew's disgusting Spike Milligan book?

I'll tell you.

Andrew's great interest was collecting fossils. He had, proudly displayed on a shelf in his Swedish pine-look bedroom, three pieces of rock with barely distinguishable 'leaf imprints', and two other pieces of rock he claimed, wrongly – but who was I to disillusion him? – were fragments of dinosaur bone. Behind these neatly labelled treasures were his 'Sunday Times

Fossil Hunter's Pull-out Poster' and his 'Pictorial Knowledge: The Great Dinosaurs' poster. His most cherished dream in the world was to find some vast fragment of Tyrannosaurus in a cornfield, the mummified head of Brontosaurus inches down in the topsoil of the recreation ground, a complete skeleton of Pterodactyl in a patch deep in the woods. Such were his aspirations, unfounded in realism.

This was the basis of my simple ploy.

As Angus was falling asleep that first night, on the lower bunk of the Swedish log cabin-look bunk-bed, I disclosed to him fabulous stories of dinosaur fragments recently found in nearby woods. Experts, I explained, thought there were probably entire Brontosauri ('Yes, Angus, Brontosauruses') there. I instructed him with a military faith to detail as to where this potential fossil hunter's El Dorado was, and, holding the electric lamp into his bleary, podgy, sleep-encrusted face, made him repeat the exact route to me.

'That's right, Angus. Isn't that interesting? You can go to sleep now. Good night!'

'Mummy's got the labour,' he burbled as he sank back into his sleep.

Angus was not the slightest bit interested in fossils. Angus was not interested in very much at all, because he was not in any sense a bright child with an inquisitive, inquiring mind. His inability to find himself an interest or hobby was a cause of concern with Alice who felt that children should be interested in things. Angus's one great interest – though Alice might have failed to notice it – was currying favour with others. So he could be relied upon in his eagerness to find a friend to go running to Andrew first thing in the morning to tell him about the fossil finds. And very likely he would pretend that the information was strictly his own which, obviously, would serve my purposes well by eliminating any risk of Andrew – who did have a modicum of intelligence – guessing that I was setting him up. It worked perfectly.

Breakfast could not end quickly enough for our intrepid explorers. Egg dribbled down Angus's face as he quivered in the excitement of a successful act of sycophancy. They were off, furtively trying to conceal the Junior Explorer Kit in the hope that I wouldn't guess where they were going. Once outside in the road the kit was strapped to Angus's back; he was, as so often, to be the donkey of the expedition.

I was still seated at the breakfast table, taking breakfast at a dignified and gentlemanly pace. 'You're not going bird-watching then?' Mavis asked.

'No, I think I'll stay in and read today,' I replied, watching Christine leaving to go upstairs and change into her bikini.

'You're really quite an intellectual!' Mavis laughed. 'And what are you reading?'

'*Gulliver's Travels*,' I lied. To her it would sound innocuous enough, a children's book. Not of course that it is any such thing. I was in fact reading Freud's paper, 'Some Psychical Consequences of the Anatomical Distinction Between the Sexes'.

No one said it, but then it didn't need to be said: my younger brother Angus was far from being an intellectual. In the normal course of events this might not have been too great a problem. But with myself always present for comparison, with my example always to follow, Alice and Ken were increasingly worried as the years were to pass about Angus and his astonishing inability to do well in anything at school. Like most parents they made a point of saying, 'One should never compare one child with another; it's not fair.' Dr Spock probably had something to say on that. Often Ken and Alice's arguments on this subject (though an argument was rarely confined to one subject: they jumped with huge generalisations to any point of attack believing, as people often do, that victory on one score constitutes an overall conquest) started with the discussion of me and my prodigious academic successes. Then, inevitably, they moved down the line to the converse matter of my little brother's failures. All in all, one way and another, Angus had a lot to thank me for. I was the apple of Ken and Alice's eye; singled out for praise by my teachers, awarded prizes. It was to continue so: winning my scholarship to Oxford . . .

Andrew and Angus were off to uncover prehistoric mysteries. Harry Richards was off to work with his briefcase and sheepskin car-coat (yes, even in this weather – 'You never know', Mavis would say), and after lunch Mavis herself would be gone to visit Alice in hospital. The whole afternoon would be free of them.

The three days gaped before me. Christine lay on her yellow Lilo and I trotted back and forth to the house to fetch her drinks. We were to talk about many things: about horses and the Pony Club meeting she had next week; about books (I had read *Brave New World*); and about love.

5

Private Worlds

I came across Andrew one day, playing with his toys in the quaint, picaresque world of his imagination. 'Mr Pitkin!' he was saying, 'Mr Pitkin, where are the Knobblies? What are they doing?' I watched with disgust. 'Wonga-wonga!' He now addressed a pitifully beaten old golliwog he had inherited from Christine's collection. 'The Knobblies are invading!'

He made a trumpet fanfare noise, then thrust a small menagerie of beetles and spiders he had obtained from Christmas crackers and Jamboree bags across the crazy-paved patio in the direction of the one-eyed golliwog. He made a series of hisses and growls.

'What are you doing, Andrew?' I inquired.

He went bright red and started stuttering. He knew he was supposed to have grown out of games like this: I had told him so. I had warned him, 'If you are still playing childish games like that it is the sign of a feeble mind. I am seriously worried about you, Andrew.' He looked frightened. I had been reading selections from Burton's *Anatomy of Melancholy*.

I no longer played like this. I had discovered how easy it was to manipulate the real world.

Daniel Porter came to me during a maths lesson and pleaded with me to give him the answers to the questions. 'Give?' I had said. Everything has a price; Ken had taught me this.

'But what can you do for me?' I asked. He looked confused

and blustered, searching round the classroom in trepidation. 'Well? How can you make it worth my while?'

'What do you want?'

I took my time.

'Come on! Shithead's coming round.'

I wore my well-we'll-have-to-see business man's expression.

'Please,' he squirmed. Ken had said: never let the customer know you're too keen to sell. I glanced at his sheet of paper: it was empty. He knew I had all the answers and that they were correct. He knew I knew this.

'Please! Come on!'

'Put Norman Edwards's bicycle under his dad's car wheels so he runs over it.' He looked suspicious. But he was desperate not to have to stay behind after lessons again.

'Okay.'

'Don't be seen. Tomorrow. They eat lunch in the back room at one-fifteen. Then.' I insisted we shake hands, then gave him the answers.

The next day, a Saturday, I situated myself in the trees opposite Norman's house at ten past two, which allowed five minutes' leeway for Mr Edwards to get into his car to drive to the football, a home match. I could see the brand new bicycle at the rear of the car, invisible from the perspective of the house. Norman had not ceased for the last fortnight (the period of time he had owned it) to remind me of the fact that his new bicycle had a three-speed gear. I felt this to be a kind of moral purgation: he was to be reminded of the transience of material possessions.

As usual, at precisely two-fifteen, having finished the bowl of sherry trifle that always completed Saturday lunch, Mr Edwards left the house, got into his car and began to reverse down the drive. Mr Edwards drove fast: he was a man who put five star petrol into a car that only needed three star, because it gave him the illusion that he drove a sports car. This was his fantasy, part of his grandiose imagined world of playboy-style living, and strictly inappropriate to the actual condition of his life. He too was to be punished for his infantile delusions. He revved the engine for a while, sending clouds of exhaust across the garden; he always did this. Mrs Edwards would be sitting inside, or just beginning to clear up the lunch – it was not possible to see because there were venetian blinds in every window. Perhaps they hid the shame and suffering she felt as her husband played his fast car games on the drive. She had endured these games every day since their marriage, an oddly unhappy pairing which I was later to discover originated in the aftermath of her conceiving Norman. (I compared the date on their marriage certificate with the date of Norman's birth – it was not difficult.) Their life together was an affair of sad and tawdry misery: she was desperately fat and unglamorous, and thus singularly inappropriate as a prop in his fantasy world. As, by rights, was his car, a Ford Escort.

He accelerated back. The bicycle of which Norman was so proud passed under the rear axle before Mr Edwards had even heard the sound of buckling metal. The handlebar became entangled in the transmission shaft and was quickly drawn up around it. The gears made a deep, thanatoid noise. The racing saddle engaged itself with the silencer and as the car continued another four yards down the drive ripped the entire exhaust system from the underbelly of the Escort. Mr Edwards leapt out of the car.

Norman's fingers were parting two slats of the venetian blind. He usually stood there to watch Daddy drive away. Through the double glazing he had heard nothing. Why, he might have been thinking, was Daddy bright red and running towards the house? Perhaps he had forgotten his blue and white scarf or the log-book he recorded mileage and the times of journeys in. Why was he crossing the flowerbed rather than coming by the path?

Mr Edwards had started to take off the belt from his trousers before reaching the door. His trousers drooped down, exposing his underwear as he thrust his hands into the pockets in search of the door key. Then he remembered that he had left the keys in the car. He seemed to hesitate as if uncertain whether to go back and fetch them. But no: Mr Edwards was an impatient man, a raging bull when roused. He hammered on the door with his fist, and as the door shook Mrs Edwards's toy poodle howled at him through the frosted glass. She had followed the dog to the door to let her husband in, but not fast enough to prevent him hammering on it again and breaking the frosted glass that showered over her and the poodle just as she fumbled with the latch. The door swung open, knocking her over so that she rolled across the floor and struck her head on the brass dwarf door-stop.

Norman had already begun to run into the kitchen.

Why did I hate them so much? Mr Edwards with the Ford Escort he fantasised into a Maserati, his wife tearfully sighing over Mills & Boon romances and helping her friend who drove meals-on-wheels to decrepit local pensioners. And Norman? Why did I hate him when perhaps I should have felt sorry for him? I knew that his life was far more miserable than mine, that his father beat him and smashed up his Airfix models when he was angry with the world, with its failure to match up to his desires. Norman was sincere, well-meaning and consistently generous with what little he had. I could remember the time he gave me his Thunderbird 3 to make my collection complete. It was the only one he had. He was the only child I knew who was so preternaturally generous. An auntie gave him a pound of Liquorice Allsorts and his first thought was to come round and share them with me. He emptied them out of the box and divided them equally, each different sort, returning mine to the box and placing his own in an old polythene bag he had brought for the purpose. It was pathetic: he had been so keen to see that I knew him to be fair that he had not even removed the polythene wrapping from the box before seeing me. The truth was, he was mercilessly sycophantic.

Something indelible in his psychological make-up forced him perpetually to demean himself before others of stronger will. He was spaniel-like in his devotions, never remonstrative however savagely he was treated. He made even the wheedling and soullessness of Angus seem like forceful self-assertion. His expectation that the world would punish him was so powerful it was like an insistent request, a masochistic demand. His mother too — she shared the existence of Mr Edwards with Norman, perhaps this was at the root of it — seemed to expect punishment. But whereas she so clearly received gratification from moaning and feeling martyred (like Alice, Alice did that too), Norman never complained, never seemed to want the happiness of indulging in self-pity. He simply expected the world to punish him, and through the medium of myself it did, unflaggingly.

He came to me once with five pounds that he had saved from his birthday present money. 'What should I do with it?' he asked.

I tormented him at first. 'What do *you* think, Norman?'

'Well, like, Mum said I should put it in the Post Office.'

'Saving money is bourgeois.' I had been reading *A Handbook of Marxism*.

'Yeah, of course,' he cowered.

'Spend it on drugs.' He looked terrified. He had heard stories about drugs, long plaintive homilies from his mother whose heart went out to all the misguided and unhappy people in the world. 'That way you will liberate your subconscious from the yoke of reality.' He nodded, his head wobbling like one of those dogs you see in the backs of people's cars.

'Er, I, well, like, I don't – '

'You don't know where to get a deal?'

'Yeah, I mean, not right now, like a good one I mean, like – '

'Leave it to me,' holding out my hand for his five dog-eared one pound notes.

'Yeah, that's the best thing, thanks Paul, it's really er . . . '

I put the money into *my* Post Office Savings Account and a week later handed him five multi-vitamins wrapped in tissue paper in a matchbox. He was undoubtedly to flush them down the lavatory or bury them somewhere for fear of detection.

'Yeah, huh, like, amazing, er, psychedelic . . . '

He was beaten so badly I could hear the screams through the smashed panes of the front door. His screams and Mrs Edwards's screams, in soprano counterpoint, 'Keith, you'll hurt him! Please, Keith!' Norman choked out his yelps in the interstices between his pump action tears and the brutal, beautiful swish of the belt.

It was to be a few years before Norman had another bicycle, when he had saved up two years' worth of his paper round money. It took him this long because I 'taxed' him. He seemed happy to pay this tax. It was as if it were a way of alleviating the burden of guilt he felt for being such an unprepossessing person, a fact that all the local kids informed him of through various means: punching him in the face, throwing him in the stinging nettles, etc.

He came round on Sunday mornings with the tax and always began, 'Sorry, er, like.'

'That's okay, Norman. What can I do for you?'

'Er, huh, I brought the money . . .'

'Oh, lovely. Thanks. You needn't have bothered to come out in the rain.'

'Er, I don't mind, like . . .'

The truth was, I was his best friend.

6

Love

In the afternoon, the moment lunch was finished – fish fingers, peas and mashed potato, lots of tomato ketchup – Andrew and Angus were out of the house again, returning to 'the site'.

'How's the bird-watching going?' I had asked, slicing a fish finger.

'Er, oh, not bad at all. Saw a – a kingfisher, and erm . . . '

I had stopped bothering to listen to Andrew's lies. Angus appeared very impressed by them, nodding his head ferociously with each bird Andrew mentioned. They were happy in their search for the dinosaur, happy too in their furtive sense of doing something I didn't know about. Really, I was doing them a favour.

Everything was working perfectly: there were minor complications suspected after the delivery and Mavis said it would be better if I didn't visit the hospital yet. She, of course, was going to.

'She's not really very poorly, you mustn't worry yourself. Poor thing, I can see how much you've been worrying.' She looked at me with great compassion. I struggled to put a brave face on during this time of great worry for all of us. 'You are a brave boy. Mummy will be so proud of you, and your father too when he gets back. Very brave.' Swallowing hard, she squeezed my arm to show how she was with me all the way.

Her eyes were watering. I could smell the rodent smell.

And that was the other thing: there was still no sign of Ken, and Mavis had been completely unable to find out where he was. She had phoned the office and they had said he could be in any hotel in Manchester, they didn't know which. Mavis must have rung dozens: she was on the phone half the night claiming it was a matter of life and death (she covered the receiver with her hand, winked at me, and said, 'It's not really'), so as to keep Directory Enquiries hard at work on a list of Manchester hotels, boarding houses, guest houses and bed-and-breakfasts. But she had no luck. She went to our house and rifled through Ken's 'home office', even feeling around down the back of the couch that Ken said did perfectly well as a spare bed, trying to find something that might tell her where he was. Again she was gripping my arm. 'I hope nothing has *happened*,' she said.

Nothing had happened. I knew this. I had taken the precaution of removing from Ken's filing cabinet the one document that pertained to his whereabouts, which was not Manchester, or even near it.

'You mustn't worry yourself, Paul,' Mavis said, rubbing her hand over my scalp. 'I'm sure everything is all right. It's been quite a time for you these last few days, hasn't it? I'm sure everything will be all right.'

'I'm sure it will, Auntie Mavis.' She had told me to call her 'Auntie': it brought us closer.

It was the third day. Mavis was off to the hospital. 'Remember, help yourself to anything you want, won't you? And if Bananas asks, give him some water. He gets through a lot in this hot weather. But don't feed him – he's bound to ask. Christine will take care of that. Cheerio! I'll send your love to Mummy.'

And she was gone.

I looked through the kitchen hatch: Bananas the spaniel, old, grey and smelling, was asleep by the sofa. Bananas was so old now that he suffered from permanent, irremovable halitosis, his mouth an awful pit of rancid organic matter. Because of this no one loved him as once they had; no one cuddled up to him any more, burying their head in his soft, shaggy neck, saying, 'Banaarhners you old thing!' That was what they had said when he was still a relatively young thing, without the stench. He was like an aged retainer or secretly loathed elderly relative everyone kept trying to persuade to go into 'a home'.

They imagined he'd die soon so they stuck with him. It was not discussed, but it was becoming apparent that if he didn't hurry up and die he'd have to be helped on his way. I was wondering about all the ways they'd express this need; how they would talk about the pain he was suffering, perhaps even believing it themselves, when it was clear to me that the only pain he suffered was occasioned by their rebuffing his shows of affection. I pictured their nostalgic reminiscences of Bananas, going through the album of Bananas snapshots saying things like, 'Do you remember that time he got the bone stuck in the fence?' 'Oh yes! That was funny!' 'He was a sweetie-pie!'

In point of fact it was not to be too long before Bananas was 'put to sleep', dying in euphemism just as he had lived in it: the 'little mistakes' when he sprang on to the Parker Knoll and pissed to show how happy he was, or heaved forth his gut-load of Chum into baby Christine's cot; the time he was 'a bit frisky today' with the leg of one of Mr Richard's fellow freemasons.

The last two afternoons had been spent by the pool, the weather remorselessly good. My examinations of Christine's anatomy had been thorough and engrossed. I became obsessed with seeing what lay beneath the thin blue triangles of her bikini top. I loved the ripples of puppy fat on her tummy when she sat up and made the Lilo dip beneath her so the water trickled over the yellow plastic. I was beguiled by the smells of shampoo discernible on the inside of her bathing cap, of chlorine after she had swum, of her sun-tan lotion like some heady tropical flower. These smells were so beautiful I was nauseated when I thought of other people's smells: Ken's slim panatella smell; Bananas; Mavis and the texture of her skin like chamois leather. All these smells connoted age and decay.

I was standing on the patio. Everyone was absent, including the still untraced and increasingly worried-over Ken. Ken was untraced because I had hidden the discovered document beneath the green foam of one of Alice's flower arrangements, a splay of dried hydrangeas with *Pernettya mucronata*, one of Alice's proudest creations. The flower arrangements were inviolable, particularly this one, placed dead centre of the dining table.

I had discovered the letter under *P* in Ken's filing system, along with a collection of other entirely innocent letters from Dave Packman. It was, in actuality, from Dave's secretary Sheila. The next day, under guise of helping Mavis in her fruitless quest for Ken, I had rung Dave's office to inquire if he knew where Ken was. He didn't. Then, with a child's natural curiosity, I asked who it was I had spoken to? Where was Miss Hibbard? And chuckling, patronising Dave informed me that she was on holiday, adding, 'You young devil!' He imagined that I had some juvenile crush on his secretary.

Ken and Sheila were having a dirty weekend in Littlehampton.

I walked down on to the lawn and, unable to see Christine, stood on the patio barbecue so as to command a panoramic view of the pool. At the deep end the yellow Lilo tapped methodically against the edge. Her Penguin *Brave New World* and her dainty make-up bag lay upon it. There was a slight, almost evaporated trail of water running across the tiles to the point where her flip-flops had been.

I was in my swimming trunks, bearing *The Last Plays of William Shakespeare*, as I walked over the vigorously Qualcastered lawn. I was reading *The Tempest* so as to be able to tell Christine about the play from which the title of her book came. I got as far as the Wendy house, now converted into Harry's potting shed where he kept the lawnmower, various pristine garden tools, and a small stack of mildly pornographic magazines no one knew about. I could hear the distant click-clock of the horse's hooves on the brick outside the stable. She'd be grooming him.

On the far side of the pool I clambered up through Mavis's 'rock garden', a paltry assemblage of a few withered plants and a handful of skull-sized boulders Harry had been ordered to arrange. The rock garden was a constant source of dispute between Harry and Mavis. He had objected to having it in the first place and so refused to water it. Mavis was too lazy to water it. So as the hot summer progressed it died.

At the top of the sloping bank I had a clear view of Christine and the horse through the foliage of the horse chestnuts. She was brushing its radiantly shiny coat, the muscles of her back undulating as she stretched from neck to rump with each stroke. It was a little like Keith Edwards, Norman's father, T-cutting and waxing his Escort. After a while she walked round and faced the horse. Their noses touched and she seemed to be whispering something to it. It moved only its tail to flick away the clusters of gathering flies. I wondered what she was saying to it. It would undoubtedly be something similar to the mawkishly sentimental film of *Black Beauty* we all went to one afternoon when it rained. Alice, Mavis and Christine all cried. I had reflected on the interesting disparity between this and the fact that they were quite happy to come home and feed Bananas a bloody great bowl of dead horse.

She was nuzzling her face against the horse's neck where the thick veins stuck out. I was fixated by the sight of her delicately constructed bottom. She stood now on an upturned bucket at the horse's side and threw her right leg over the animal's back. The flip-flop was dispatched into a thicket of grass beyond the courtyard. I recalled Mavis telling her she must not ride bareback. Christine was now on the brink of transgressing that edict. The second flip-flop fell from her foot, she shook the reins, and the horse trotted – pad pad – into the field.

'Go on boy,' she said.

The horse was cantering up and down the field, stopping at the edge of the long grass, turning, coming back to the chestnut trees where I sat, unseen. As he moved away small pods of dust plummeted up from his hooves. Christine emitted little cries of excitement as he went faster and faster, then, in the final act of her transgression against Mavis, drove the animal on into the long grass. 'There's all sorts of old junk in there,' Mavis had warned, 'he'll catch his leg on something.' Christine galloped now, the long grass piling up around them as high as her naked and clinging feet.

Then, as inevitably must happen, there was the sound of her screaming and the riderless horse was bending nonchalantly to look at its fallen mistress. I was already running frantically across the rocky paddock. Into the long grass, its abrasive tongues licking over my skin.

When I found her she was lying on her back on a wave of

flattened grass. 'Paul!' she said, gasping and catching her breath. 'I'm so glad you heard me.'

'Are you hurt?' I was kneeling at her side. There were tears in her eyes.

'I don't think so, not too bad.' I was very happy. I was resting my hands on her ankles. She was wiping the grey streaks of tears and toy-mascara from her face. 'Oh, Paul,' she sighed, trembling. I was overjoyed. Then she rolled over in the grass, crying a little yelp of pain as her sore knee scraped the ground. Another wave of grass crashed down. 'My back, I think it's bruised. Can you see?'

There were little pieces of dead grass embedded in her back. I ran my fingers over it. 'No, lower down, lower down,' she said. I could feel the elastic rim of the bikini bottom against my wrists. I could smell the smell of the horse emanating up from her. 'Give me a massage,' she giggled, and I started kneading the flesh above her bottom. 'Lower down,' she said, admonishing me to greater daring. She started wiggling and laughing. 'Don't! I'm ticklish!' she squealed. I tickled her.

This went on for a short while, then she rolled over and spoke in her deeper, playing-at-adults voice. 'You can kiss me if you like,' she said, and pouted her smudged red lips. We kissed and I attempted to place my small hand inside her bikini top. For a few moments she raised no objections to this. Then the game was terminated as abruptly as it had begun. 'Right,' she said, leaping up, 'that's all we're doing today.' And she proceeded to march off through the long grass. I followed. I was strangely obedient to her instructions.

We were by the swimming pool when Mavis returned an hour or so later. She deposited herself on the white tiles so the marigold slacks were stretched taut over her fat legs. 'I've got super news for you,' she told me, and I knew it would be disappointing. It was. Ken had returned from his 'business trip' and Alice was so much better she'd be out of hospital within a couple of days. 'Then you can see your baby sister,' Mavis continued. 'I bet you're looking forward to that.'

'Yes. I am glad Mummy's well. Where's Daddy? Is he here now?'

And he was. Ken was emerging through the french windows

and lumbering down across the lawn. He was waving and smiling.

'I was just telling your dad what a job we had looking through his office to try and find out where he was.'

I looked up at Ken. He was radiantly happy and coming across the tiles to pick me up and ruffle my hair as he always did when he'd been away for a few days. The full significance of Mavis's remark had not yet dawned on him. He would not be radiantly happy when it did.

7

Cross-purposes

I'm four. Ken and I are kicking a ball about in the garden. He's dribbling the ball round the Christmas trees. 'Tackle!' he tells me. But I don't. I'm trying to position him so that when he strikes towards goal I can duck out of the way and the ball will soar up to the patio and Angus's pram.

Another day we're playing soldiers: Ken has an old cricket bat he proudly tells me he used when he played for the County under-15s, and is pretending it is a machine gun, rattling his tongue against the roof of his mouth. I have to oblige by returning fire with the plastic ray-gun he's bought me. He falls on the lawn clutching his belly.

Later Angus is old enough to join in. Again I'm trying to work Ken up into a frenzy of joy in which he will accidentally use his great bulk to injure Angus. He's like a lumbering robot in my hands as he dashes for the ball and his size eleven shoe comes down on Angus's frail leg. And Angus falls, erupting into tears.

* * * * * * *

Ken almost tore the office apart when he discovered that Sheila's letter was gone. It was a couple of days after his return home, and I was standing outside the door listening to him charging round the room snorting through dilated nostrils.

Alice being still in hospital, it was his job to get dinner for Angus and me, but the shock of his discovery had completely put this out of his mind. Angus was watching television, a commercial for a new toy he would be bound to want. He was gawping with his usual TV passivity. 'Why isn't Daddy making dinner?' he asked.

'Daddy's just finishing some important business,' I smiled.

Some time passed before I returned to the office door, knocked and entered. Ken was pink and beaded with perspiration. The room smelt of it. 'Is there something wrong, Daddy?' I inquired.

A mumble of ums and ers came out, expressing the loss of 'something'. Then he remembered he was supposed to have cooked dinner, started fidgeting violently, and proceeded through to the kitchen.

The kitchen on that day was as if designed by a malicious Heath Robinson with a powerful personal vendetta against Ken. The pan for the frozen peas boiled over and splashed all over the grilling chops, which spat their fat all over his trousers. He went to wipe them clean, only to discover that he had forgotten to wring out the cloth after using it at lunch to wipe up the Golden Syrup Angus had spilt. He grew increasingly irate and donned Alice's apron. Then struggled with the packet of instant mash and spilt it all over the floor. The bits kept crunching under his feet, each crackle adding to his rage and frustration. Alice would have been delighted to see this vivid confirmation of what she was always telling me — that men just didn't understand how difficult the housework could be.

Finally, when things were under a moderate degree of control, Ken broached the subject that weighed so heavily upon his mind. 'Paul, I wonder,' he began, patting me on the shoulder. 'You helped Mrs Richards look through my office.'

'Yes, Daddy.'

'You didn't happen to notice — you're so observant I thought you might have done — er, whether or not — ' It was blissful: he was grovelling to me. ' — she, did she move anything? A letter or anything.' And then he tried to make light of it by snorting, 'You know how absent-minded she is!'

I laughed too.

'Yes, Daddy,' I replied. 'Well, I think she found something that she thought might be useful in your suit pocket. I'm not sure exactly what it was.'

One of the chops was on fire.
Angus stood in the doorway whining. 'I'm hungey, Dad.'
Ken had gone quite white.
'It's coming!' he yelled at Angus. 'Coming coming coming!' He was angry. 'Go and sit down, will you?'
He fought to extinguish the blazing pork chop.
Angus ran away into the living-room.
Throughout dinner Ken attempted to come to terms with the fact that he had been stupid enough to leave Sheila's letter in his pocket. For that was the only plausible explanation he could come up with. Which was as I intended.

In point of fact I had not actually lied to him: Mavis had found a letter in Ken's suit pocket. It was not the same letter, but then I hadn't claimed that it was. Ken's paranoid imagination had done that.
 I knew Mavis had found the letter and I knew what it said. It was I who had planted it there for her to find. I had chanced upon this document during the afternoon of the first day spent at Harry and Mavis's house. I was conducting a routine search of the house, scrutinising, amongst other things, Harry's diary, letters from Mavis's senile grandmother and the family photograph album, a volume of particular interest. It was a sort of potted history of the Richards's married life. There was a photograph of Harry holding a young Christine aloft, with Bananas jumping up and flailing his long pink tongue. *Harry & Christine in the garden 1963*, Mavis had written beneath it. Another was entitled *Harry & Mr Long 1958*, and showed a noticeably younger Harry on some proud occasion when he had obviously succeeded in ingratiating himself with a business superior. He seemed to drip Brylcream. *Bananas chasing birds Granny's 1965* showed a youthful Andrew with a stick in his hand during his Tarzan the Apeman period, when he was wont to climb up trees and make a pathetic yodelling noise. I remembered it only too well. Yet another was called *Paul watching the kids horsing around! 1966*, and featured a serious-looking me looking on at the childish antics of a number of my peers. I was particularly pleased by the way Mavis had singled me out from the vulgar mass, even at the tender age of six.
 I proceeded from this to a leisurely perusal (Christine was

sunbathing on the Lilo) of Harry's diary. It was concealed between the pages of this diary that I discovered the letter, more a note in fact, that was to give the impetus to my plan. It was a very simple document, unmistakably in Harry's ill-formed handwriting. It read: 'Sorry I couldn't catch you today. Don't let Mavis know about it whatever you do. I know you wouldn't, Harry.' Its very ambiguity — the possible range of interpretations that could be imposed upon it — was the basis of my plan.

Mavis, like Ken, had a mind quick to jump to conclusions. She also distrusted secrets. And most important — without this my whole scheme might have failed — she was increasingly worried as she grew older, fatter, and less attractive that Harry might start looking around for 'a younger woman'. (I had heard her discussing this with Alice in, of course, somewhat veiled terms.)

Thus, when she found this note she became immediately suspicious.

A few days after Alice's return from hospital we were all to have dinner together. Christine came round early to help Alice with the cooking. This killed two birds with one stone by helping Christine with her school domestic science (learning to be a housewife) course, and demonstrating to Alice how critically aware everyone was of the greatly debilitating deed she had performed in giving birth to baby Rachel.

After we had eaten I got Ken out into the garden by telling him the smell of smoke was making Alice feel poorly. Anything that upset Alice was sacred at this point — it was her time of dominion. I wondered how long it would be before the novelty of her giving birth wore off and she had to cast about for new nervous complaints and illnesses.

'Naughty girl!' Mavis said, whispering even though Alice had gone upstairs with the baby and was well beyond earshot. 'Suffering in silence again.' She tutted as though reprimanding the dog.

Alice was a great one for 'suffering in silence'. It was an ominous silence punctuated with enfeebled little coughs, and quiet *ohh* noises she contrived to drop into gaps in the conversation, where they would have the optimum effect in calling attention to her silent pain. They were invariably accompanied by the raising of her hand to her left breast, a simulation of the silently suffered agonies of heartburn (or — who knows? — something worse), and by a wrinkling of the forehead she might have learnt from the martyred, gazing-towards-heaven expression of the arrow-filled St Sebastian.

'That's very thoughtful of you, Paul,' Ken grunted.

'Isn't it? So thoughtful, thinking of your mum like that!' Mavis said. She'd have her cigarette in the garden too. As she followed Ken towards the french windows she stopped and squeezed my arm. 'That's right. You take care of your mum.' She was wearing a great deal of perfume.

Harry had gone out to look at the car which had been 'playing up', so there were only Andrew and Christine left. Angus was upstairs in bed. I told Andrew about a book Angus had found containing an article about fossils. He was bounding off up the stairs to ask Alice if he could go and visit Angus. Which left me all alone with Christine.

She looked a little embarrassed. It was the first time we had seen each other since kissing in the long grass. I put my hand around her waist and went to kiss her. She leapt up saying, 'Someone might come in.'

I assured her they wouldn't.

'They're only just out in the garden,' she said, pointing at Ken and Mavis.

'They'll be a while yet,' I said.

This had the effect of enraging her. 'How d'you know that?' she almost shouted. 'You really think you're clever don't you? Well, I don't.'

I enjoyed her impetuous, sulking anger. I strolled towards the Parker Knoll. 'It's a logical deduction,' I said. 'Shall I explain?'

She grunted in a faintly conciliatory way.

'Well, firstly they're still smoking.'

'Very clever.' I liked her sarcasm.

'And secondly, I know what they're talking about.'

'Really believe you,' she said. 'I hate you.'

I knew this was not true.

'I do know,' I said, and touched her bottom.

'Get off! You're just saying that. Show-off.' She was a nice pink colour. I said nothing. 'What are they talking about then? If you're so clever.'

I had picked up the newspaper and was filling in the crossword.

'You *don't* know. Do you?'

'Don't be histrionic, Christine. It's so unbecoming in you. I'm afraid I don't think I ought to tell you what they're talking about.'

This had the desired effect. 'Oh yeah! Reckons!' She now performed the action used by many of her school fellows. She beat her hand against the side of her face. It was a way of saying she thought I was stupid. Then she scratched her chin in a very ostentatious manner. This was supposed to signify incredulity.

I remained perfectly calm.

I did in fact know what Ken and Mavis were talking about. Here is a précis of their conversation, as summary as is concomitant with a clear explanation of what was said:

K: Mavis, did you find a letter in my suit pocket?
M: Yes, Ken, I did.
K: Do you intend telling Alice about it?
M: No. (*She guesses now that the note refers to a secret surprise Ken and Harry are planning for Alice.*)
K: That's very good of you. (*He goes on to ask if he could have the note back and Mavis informs him that she has put it back. She has, but I have removed it.*)

Satisfied, for the moment, with the outcome of their conversation, they were returning at a gentle pace up the garden; Ken happy in the knowledge that Mavis would not tell Alice about his affair, Mavis happy that Harry's note did not refer to his having an affair. And all because of the remarkable ambiguity and lack of explicit reference they both employed in their conversation. I was jubilant with the total misunderstanding of circumstances I had managed to achieve. Christine, ignorant of all this, was far from jubilant. She was getting very cross.

'You DON'T know what they're talking about!'
'There's no need to shout.'
'Wasn't.'
'Don't be angry, my sweetheart.'

'Uuuurrrrrr!' Which was to indicate she did not think of herself as my sweetheart.

'You are behaving badly today.'

'Tell me then. Go on.'

'It would be better if I didn't.'

'Can't!' she snapped.

'I can,' I explained, 'but it will cause you pain.'

'Reckons.' And she took to scratching her chin again.

I made her plead for a while longer. I made her promise that if I told her she would not, under any circumstances, tell anyone else. With each promise I extracted she grew more and more impatient. Finally, with Ken and Mavis no more than ten yards short of the french windows, I conceded and agreed to tell her. On condition that I could touch her breasts. This she granted, a little reluctantly, and pulled away after the briefest of touches. 'Now, you've got to tell me,' she demanded. 'You promised.'

So I told her. 'Your mother and my father are having a love affair.'

Her eyes opened wide in disbelief.

'You mean . . . ?'

I nodded gravely.

Ken and Mavis were on the patio.

8

Medicine Cabinet

I disliked Alice when she was feeling sorry for herself, which was most of the time. I disliked, for instance, the way she would tell me how many of my nappies she had had to wash as she leant over my pram or peered at me harnessed like a mini-Michelin man in my pushchair. I could never think what I was supposed to do about it — I had the sensation even then of being merely some kind of two-dimensional prop in her world. Later she did the same with Angus, and I became a conspirator with her. She would tell me — I was good, I no longer dirtied nappies and never wet the bed (I learnt quickly) — how many of Angus's nappies she had washed. She was pegging them to the line and I was trotting round on the patio. She spoke of him as of an object. There was in all this that same kind of relish she took in chewing bitter things like the slices of lime. As though the pain and dirt were purging her.

'Angus has wet the sheets,' she told me with glee. I had not: we were ganging up.

It was the same with heavy shopping bags. She'd bring them in from the car and say, 'Feel how heavy that is.' I'd tug at the bag full of tins of Heinz baby-mush or big red cans of Cow & Gate milk with a picture of a baby wearing a crown on them. She would count out the Heinz tins, building a little mountain like those in the supermarket. The message was loud and clear: *All this is for you. Now, don't you feel guilty?*

When I was big enough to help carry the bags the message was for Angus, and Alice and I were conspirators.

Sometimes I was on the landing and would watch through the half-open bathroom door (deliberately half-open), as she gloated over the contents of the medicine cabinet in her worst, her deepest and most ugly self-pity. These were the times when we were closest, odd as it is to recall. I would trot through into the bedroom where she had laid out a selection of her medications on the white candlewick bedspread. Without her asking I knew what she wanted. I said, 'What's that one for, Mummy?' and she told me which of her fictional ailments that potion was for. We played this game a full half-hour sometimes, Alice telling me about various symptoms, where the pain was worst, and so forth. Then, as if I had gratified her, almost – I was not aware of this at the time – as if I had satisfied some sexual need, she would kiss and cuddle me. These were the times when we were most intimate. It always smelt of cough linctus and plasters.

There were moments of intimacy like this with Ken as well, though they were never the same moments. They were private too. There never was a time when either of them openly expressed affection in front of the other. Similarly they never, knowingly, performed more than the most perfunctory and dry kiss in front of me. For a time I thought this was all they ever did, until one day I looked on from one of my hiding places as Ken slid his hand into Alice's blouse and played with her breasts. The nylon was like cling-film on his knuckles.

My closest moments with Ken were either in the garden when he would lift me up and swing me round (there was a smell of cut grass and earth), or last thing at night after Alice had put me to bed. He would come in to say good night and tickle me and we would pretend to fight. There was a short period during which he tried to read me bedtime stories. He read clumsily and was often embarrassed by his attempts at characterising the people in the stories. His Little Red Riding Hood, for example, was risible. I would generally put him out of his misery by feigning sleep and he would kiss my forehead, smelling of Scotch and slim panatellas.

Angus too had private kissing and cuddling sessions. He had a greater need of them, particularly at around this time when he had not been long at school. School was a torture for him. The first day he went to the lavatory and tugged down his little grey shorts to wee-wee. Alice had never thought to tell him that little boys didn't need to do this once they were big enough. All the other boys turned upon him. He tugged his shorts back up again. They were imploring him to take them down again. One foul creature had produced a half-sucked gobstopper from his handkerchief and was offering this as payment. Angus was terrified. The children started poking him and jostling him. One boy butted him in the chest with his head. Another produced a wet mop and systematically jabbed it behind Angus's knees until he lost his balance, tripped, then ran crying from the lavatory. He held on to his wee all day. Freud, I imagine, would have made a good deal of that experience.

By contrast, I was never bullied at school. I was not physically strong but ingratiated myself quickly with those who were. It's a relationship one often observes, among adults as well as children: the thugs enjoying the company of one person who serves as their intellectual mentor. This was the foundation of my relationship with Justin. He called me 'the Brain'.

I was once involved in a fight. Daniel Porter's older brother Matthew hated me. He had sprung on me in the playground. I was terrified. A circle of children had formed around us in seconds and were chanting their support for him. I could feel my heart beating against my rib-cage. He pushed me to the ground and jumped on my chest, pinning my arms down with his knees. He was strangling me, then punching me in the face so my mouth felt bloated and my teeth loose. The next day Justin heard about it. 'Everyone knows you don't fight,' he said. ('Brainy kids' didn't, in his conception of things.) Later that afternoon he walked up to Matthew and said, 'Your mum's a whore.' Then smashed him to pieces. It was the beginning of our campaign of attrition against that whole family.

As I say, there was very little communal intimacy in our family. Most of the time we were dour and quiet when together. An argument between Ken and Alice would be brewing up for later when we kids were out of the way. The only occasion on which there was ever any great display of mutual love was when one of us had achieved something in the outside world. When I had won a prize at school, for instance.

It was a few days after Ken and Mavis's discussion of 'the letter' (Ken had found that Mavis had not returned it to his pocket and was anxious for another chat with her) that Ken got the news of his promotion. Everyone was terribly happy about it.

If there was a time when I disliked Alice more than when she was feeling sorry for herself, it was when she was enjoying this kind of giggly, flirtatious, smug happiness. All her tiny aspirations came bubbling to the surface: new furniture, new car, new kitchen equipment and, tentatively – she did not wish to shatter the evening's peace – new house with an extra bedroom. It was to be a very long time before we got this new house. Angus and I ended up sharing my bedroom; Rachel got her own, with new bunny rabbit wallpaper. Angus had had astronaut wallpaper, being a boy.

The other news was that Ken's old job was to be taken by Norman's dad, Keith Edwards, the man so very adept in the use of his belt. 'What a small world,' Alice said, referring to the fact that he lived only just down the road.

The next day I saw Justin. He had been caught stealing from the village shop. 'I don't even like Fruit and Nut,' he told me, 'I just felt like nickin it.' This seemed to make his apprehension all the more unjust.

'The world is an unfair place,' I told him.

He grunted, picked his nose, then said, 'How comes you never get caught?'

I had given him the impression that I led a thriving criminal life. I had once stolen Mr Burton's car-keys, largely with the object of impressing this fact upon Justin. 'Just lucky, I suppose,' I said.

'No, it's more than that.' His expression indicated that he knew it was something to do with me being a 'brainy geezer'. He was peeling the insulating tape off the handlebars of his bicycle. Then he looked up. 'No one ever suspects you, no one would ever reckon on you nickin nothin.'

'Presentation, Justin,' I said. 'Image.' These were precisely the words used by Mr Burton when he was eulogising the virtues of clear and legible handwriting. Ken also spoke of presentation in the context of salesmanship.

'What d'you mean?'

So I decided to demonstrate to him.

Taking faithful old Norman with us, we headed to the village shop. Justin, of course, could not go in. The owners had felt sorry for old Mr Burrows and had come to an agreement with him which placed an indefinite ban on Justin's entering the shop. He had also been beaten by the elderly, but still vigorous, Mr Burrows.

I told him to hide in the bushes opposite the shop. He flung himself down and crawled off into the undergrowth. A small hillock covered with privet bushes afforded a good view of the shop's interior.

'You come with me,' I told Norman. He was frightened. 'Norman, if your chin keeps wobbling like that I'll have to ask Justin to drown you.' He clamped his mouth shut and we proceeded across the gravel in front of the shop.

The principle I was intent on demonstrating was that of being boldly obsequious to people. I wanted to teach Justin how to behave in the same manner. But, in fact, it was not so much a principle with me. It was more a matter of my natural disposition. I enjoyed being sycophantic. I enjoyed getting people to like me as much as possible, even when I could not foresee any immediate benefit to be gained from so doing. My ingratiating conversation was less pre-considered and less facetious than I may sometimes have implied. I got active pleasure out of my obsequiousness.

'You are creating a decoy, Norman. You will go over to the sweet counter and take some time deciding which sweets you want to purchase. Got that?'

'Er, er, Paul . . . '

'Yes? Stop shaking, Norm. Stop burbling. You know what I'll have to have done if you carry on like that.'

'Sorry, er, like, I haven't got any money. To buy the sweets, sorry.'

'Oh, Norm. Why didn't you say? There's no need to apologise. Here.' I gave him two shillings. It did not feel like a great loss: it had been his in the first place. 'Nothing ostentatious, remember.' We went into the shop.

I began immediately by ingratiating myself with the woman who ran the shop. We talked about the weather and I asked her how she was. 'Oh, struggling on, struggling on,' she told me.

She was always struggling on. I then followed an old lady called Mrs Sidney round the shop, helping her by carrying her basket and instructing her on the subject of what she should eat for her supper: a Fray Bentos pie. I told her about Alice's pregnancy, how the baby had been born premature but was very well now.

She wheeled along at her side a tartan trolley she always used for shopping so she didn't have to carry things. Into this I piled goods indiscriminately: nine-volt batteries, a dog-leash and rubber ball, a stapler, three raspberry-flavoured jellies, a picture book of the Royal Family (how consummately satisfying to have a chance of grovelling to them), a can of Kattomeat and two pounds of castor sugar. Mrs Sidney was, of course, virtually blind. I then packed the trolley for her, so covering the stolen goods without her seeing them, paid for my packet of biscuits and left the shop, wheeling the trolley for her. Norman paid for his sweets.

Walking over the gravel, I could see in the shade beneath the bushes Justin's eyes, glowing like those of an odd nocturnal animal. Norman followed us with his 9d. worth of sweets and the carefully saved 1/3 change clasped in his palm. I told Mrs Sidney how we had to walk the same way as her anyway, so I would take her shopping trolley for her. She told me what a sweet young man I was. Charming.

'What about the bikes?' Norman piped up.

'We didn't bring our bicycles today, did we, Norman?'

'Er, but – ' I was telling Mrs Sidney how the baby slept soundly and had the same pram I used to have.

I had expected that we would walk the half-mile or so to her house, but she stopped resolutely at the bus-stop and insisted she was taking the bus.

She proved to be as stubborn as a mule on this point.

'I thought you always walked when it was a nice day,' I said.

'Oh no, dear, I do feel so tired.'

The problem consisted of a man also waiting at the bus-stop who would not be blind to my emptying out the contents of the trolley. The bus was due in six minutes: I was a little frightened.

'You'll be all right then, Mrs Sidney. Goodbye then.'

'Yes dear, thank you so much.'

I waved as we carried on down the road and Norman

tentatively aped me. The man at the bus-stop looked at his wrist-watch.

Ahead of us, on the left-hand side of the road, the drains were being excavated. The hole was about twelve feet deep, a nodal point at which three drainage pipes converged and flowed into one. It was the lunch hour.

I looked round and saw Mrs Sidney and the man facing away. Justin had emerged from the undergrowth and was following us at about a hundred yards' distance.

I fell against Norman, my shoulder hitting him in the middle of the back and carrying him easily into the hole. His knee engaged itself with one of the lamps as he tumbled through the flimsy string barricade. He dragged with him, down into the drains, a considerable portion of the barricade and two of the lamps. He began to yell shortly after hitting the serrated white concrete, and one of his legs flopped over into the smooth, earthenware-like sewage vent.

The man was running from the bus-stop, Justin following him. I started crying out, 'My friend is hurt! Please! Help! Norm, Norm, are you all right?' I turned to exhort the running man. 'Quickly!' I screamed. The man had jumped down into the hole. There were tears in my eyes. 'Shall we get an ambulance?' I called.

'Yes, yes, hurry.'

I dispatched Justin to ring for the ambulance and went myself to comfort the distraught Mrs Sidney. I took the opportunity of carefully emptying the stolen goods from her trolley.

Later Justin and I were in his garden, a wild and overgrown garden filled with rusting metal, pieces of old cars, discarded radios and vacuum cleaners. He was clearing a space where we could sit amongst the brambles and five-foot-tall grass. 'Bril!' he declared. 'Who'd ave thought of lookin in the old bag's bag, er, trolley? And if they ad they'd of reckoned it was er. Magic.'

I agreed.

'Shame about Norm though,' he lamented.

I agreed again. 'Anyway, Justin, the trouble is that it's going to be some time before you can pull off a job like that. No one trusts you like they trust me.'

'Yeah. I know.'
'But you can change that.'
'Yeah?'
'You have to do something positive to demonstrate to people that you are a reformed character.'
'Yeah? Like what?'
'Like the things I do. Offer to carry old ladies' shopping for them. Join the Cub Scouts.'
'Pull the uver one. They kicked me out yonks ago.'

I remembered. Mrs Dickinson had expelled him after he threw a fellow Cub into the camp fire and so ruined the barbecue.

'Well, I'll think about it,' I told him.

9

Looking after Animals

Norman's mother, Beth, was very fat, and was one of those people who either believed she was not as fat as she was, or felt that by dressing appropriately she could force her body into a more desirable shape. Keith, her husband, was a short man who held his head high and walked with a jaunty bounce in his step, hoping that this would simulate the effect of a greater height. I saw this phenomenon all around me: Christine worried that her feet were too big and always tried to get shoes a size too small as if she could persuade her feet to fit the shoe. The Clarks lady and Mavis would work hard to persuade her to confess that she was suffering agony as she walked round the shoe shop. She would sulk and argue with the findings of the elaborate calibrator patented by Clarks. 'But your feet aren't too big, for a girl your size,' they said. 'They're perfectly normal.' She wouldn't have it.

In point of fact they were perfectly normal, whatever that is, as I too had been at pains to assure her during our anatomical class in the horse's field. I had kissed the instep of both feet.

Beth wore a bra that was a number of sizes too small for her large breasts and so forced them to protrude up into the area where, had she been so immodest, her cleavage would have displayed itself. The effect of this was that she appeared to possess a smaller, third breast that nuzzled up from between its big sisters. Norman was tormented on account of this. 'Your mum got three?' someone would shout across the playground or through the mist of an early morning as we went into school. The torment arrived in many different forms: absolutely earnest inquiries from seemingly innocent faces, 'Where exactly is the third one, have you seen them?' or, by a strange process of ramification, the automatically identifiable nickname, 'the three musketeers'.

Norman hated his mother's body for the pain it had caused him, every bit as much as she hated it for the pain it caused her.

'I think Paul must be having a good influence on Justin,' I heard Mavis telling Alice a few days later. She was referring to the fact that Justin had very thoughtfully gone to her — entirely of his own accord — to ask if she could drive Beth to the hospital after the accident. 'He does seem to be settling down. You can understand, can't you? The father, disgusting old boy. Both the brothers were louts, of course. One of them emigrated to Canada. I should think they were glad to see the back of him.'

Mavis drove the sobbing Beth to the hospital and I went to pay a quick visit on Christine. Andrew was there, playing with his plastic soldiers. 'Find those fossils yet?' I asked. He looked desperately unhappy.

Although she was crying, Beth was happy about Norman's broken leg. There was nothing she liked more than nursing the sick, and, because of his plight, she knew Keith could not possibly beat Norman for some time. Beth tucked him up in bed and brought glasses of Lucozade and ice-cream (she seemed dimly to associate this with the time Norman had his tonsils out) to build up his strength, she said. He had lost a lot of blood. It was a nice time for Norman too; he felt safe lying there in bed, the children who were usually beating him up coming and bearing gifts of old comics and swizzle-sticks as tokens of their hypocritical sympathy. Perhaps Norman even reflected that life would be better all round if his leg were permanently broken. He was always the first to leap at any opportunity for staying in bed; he'd had hysterical German measles on three occasions, the same way some women have hysterical pregnancies. Either that, or his antibodies were so weak he really had had German measles three times.

Strange to say, I had never actually been inside Keith and Beth's house before. I had stood at the door and seen the brass dwarf door-stop that Beth cut her head on the day the underbelly was ripped from the Ford Escort, but invitations to enter the house had been ominously lacking. To feed my natural curiosity I had had to rely on Norman's vague descriptions of the house's interior, apologetic mumbles invariably prefixed with, 'Well, er, it's not finished yet, like.'

'What do you mean, Norm? Be more lucid.'

'Er, like, Dad hasn't finished all the rooms yet.'

From which I gleaned only that Keith was not as avid a Do-It-Yourself man as he might once have thought he was going to be. 'If you're going to start a job, finish it.' This was one of Ken's proverbial instructive adages.

Norman lived in a room that resembled a cave. He slept on a horsehair mattress on the bare floorboards with great lumps of plaster hanging in dusty clusters from the ceiling. A single piece of grey wire sprouted from the wall to power the light that was loosely tacked to one of the rafters. Beth's hand was evident in the frilly shade that so incongruously surrounded the bulb. In the corner was the one piece of new furniture, a spotlessly white Hygena wall unit with drawers and shelves; his clothes, ironed and folded by Beth, were placed in the drawers, and what remained of the Airfix models that Keith had smashed up one night adorned the shelves; ships without masts, planes with one wing, cars without engines. Symbols, it seemed, of impotence.

His *World Encyclopaedia of the Animal Kingdom* also sat on the shelves. He would take this book down and spend hours leafing through its many pages of colour illustrations. There were animals in the jungle (the way he said 'the jungle' made it seem like one place, somewhere mysterious in Africa, as elusive as the source of the Nile or El Dorado), or animals in big green game-parks where behatted rangers drove round in black and white, zebra-camouflaged Land Rovers. There was one particular picture that always stuck in my mind: a man stood wearing a white jungle hat amidst thick and dark foliage. (The effects of chiaroscuro gave an impression of enormous wealth, of Nature's luxuriance.) At his side stood the gorilla, wrapping its thickly muscled, hairy arm around the calico man and nonchalantly chomping on a banana. It seemed to represent everything Norman saw in 'the jungle': a place of simple relationships, a millennial dream of peace and abundance. I would sneer, 'Norman you are pathetically naive. You have no idea. If the gorilla hadn't been given the banana by the man and was hungry, he'd turn round and eat the man.'

'Gorillas are vegetarian,' he said with irksome simplicity, but with no sense of triumph.

'I was speaking metaphorically, Norman. Only the abundance of bananas prevents them fighting; fodder comes before morality or so-called compassion. Read Marx.'

I was always doing this: quashing people with high-falutin intellectual references. (I still do.) With Norman I might as easily have said, 'Read Barbara Cartland.' It would have meant about the same, except he might dimly have wondered why it was his mother cried over those tomes of materialist philosophy.

There were many caves of solitude in the Edwards's household. Beth read Mills & Boon romances in the sitting-room and cried over her dreams. Norman read his animal book and cried too. The jungle was his idyllic, enchanted world. Mr Burton had everyone write about what they wanted to be when they grew up: Daniel Porter wanted to be an astronaut, Justin wanted to be a heavyweight boxer. Most of the boys wanted to be footballers (they even specified which team they wished to play for), and the girls wanted to be nurses, fashion designers, housewives and female astronauts (Mr Burton was impressed by this last). I wanted to be a nuclear physicist, and Norman vaguely wanted to 'look after animals'. 'I would like to be a vet or a zoo keeper or a ranger on a safari park in Africa,' he wrote. 'I would not mind what it was if it was to do with animals.'

I think – I do not know – that with the exception of the odd aspirant housewife, he is the only one of that class of 8-year-olds who has fulfilled his stated intentions.

I went into Norman's room followed by Beth. She was wondering, I imagine, what I – from a nice home with fitted carpets, wallpaper and flower arrangements – must think of this dungeon. Norman was lying on the mattress, his plastered leg pointing at forty-five degrees towards the venetian-blinded window. The animal book was open, arched over the plaster thigh, its pages bright with Technicolor jungle images.

'Hello, Norm! How are you?' I said. Beth sobbed and rushed out of the cave.

'Er, okay, sorry . . . ' Involuntarily it had popped out.

'Sorry? Why sorry? Is something wrong?' I had to take a tough line with this constant apologising.

'Er, I thought, I thought like . . . ' Words, logic, meaning struggled to find an exit. Justin would always say, 'What's wrong, mate? Your cakehole blocked up?'

'Here, I brought some comics for you.' (I had stolen them from Angus.)

'Oh, thanks, cheers. I'll bring them back in the morning, I –'

'No, Norman, they're for you. They're a present. Give you something to read while you're off your feet.'

He was just beginning to relax a bit when I said, 'All right if I take a seat?' which served as a horrible reminder that there were no seats. I pulled up the old tea chest he kept his toys in. 'I expect you'll be out and about in a few days. Get you a crutch to get about on, eh? You'll be as right as rain in no time.'

I noticed by the bed, stacked up in a neat pile like a little shrine, the sweets Norman had bought with the two shillings I had given him.

'What have you been reading about?'

'Oh, er, I was just kind of looking at the pictures and, er . . . '

'Yes?'

'Well, I read this bit about the, er, a kangeroo like – '

'What's this? Ah! An albino kangeroo.'

'Er yeah, that's er – '

'Yes. Do tell me, Norman. I'm very interested.'

'Yeah, the albino, an albino kangeroo is very rare like, they're . . . ' I nodded feverishly to encourage him. 'They're kind of very easy victims to, er predators like . . . '

'Yes?'

'Er, this one is even more rare, because it's got two babies, er joeys.'

'I see. Why is that so rare?' I was beginning to realise what God-like patience schoolteachers must need.

'Like, normally, the er, thing the mother – '

'Pouch.'

'Yeah, well it's normally not big enough for two and, well – '

'Or three, I suppose?' I hadn't intended the reference to Beth's bra.

'Well, no.'

'Tell me about this. Wallabies, wallaroos, potoroos, boogaries, pademelons. What on earth are they?'

'Yeah, that's like the different names for kangeroos, like different types of them. They're some really small ones, er . . .'

I leafed through the pages of the book. Norman was very happy that I was interested in it. I wondered – as an experiment – how long it would take to get him to offer it to me, this his most prized possession? Twenty seconds? Twenty-five? By one of the strange inversions of human psychology it would give him a great deal of pleasure, even as its loss pained him. He enjoyed these acts of self-denial, particularly where I, his idol, was concerned. He said, 'You can er borrow it if you like.' He was halfway there without prompting.

'No, Norman. I've got lots of books, and I can always look at it round here, when I come to visit you.'

'Er, yeah, okay.' He was delighted by my reference to future visits. He was in fact more than halfway to offering to give me the book. He was well aware what 'borrow' meant in our language. I had 'borrowed' his penknife, used it to slash Timothy Torkinghorn's bicycle tyres, then planted it in Daniel Porter's school satchel. That was borrowing.

'Would you like a sweet?' He held out the packet of wine gums from the shrine.

'That's very kind, Norman, but I won't. You have one though.'

We made no direct reference to the circumstances of the accident. He asked if we had managed to get the stuff out of Mrs Sidney's trolley and I said we had. 'Bit of a close shave,' he said, and we laughed. Whether he thought I had intentionally pushed him into the hole I did not know. It was quite apparent that it was a possibility we simply were not going to discuss. It would probably have caused him more suffering to know for sure, me being his best friend.

I read aloud from the animal book for his edification: 'The dodo', I read, 'was discovered by the Portuguese on the island of Mauritius sometime in the early 1500s. These fat and flightless birds weighed about fifty pounds and were killed off by 1681. It was not long before other species on the nearby islands were also killed off. They were as stupid and defenceless as they looked. Not even a stuffed dodo remains.'

'I'll pop round and see you tomorrow, Norm. You old dodo.'
I smiled and left.

10

Window-breaking

Eager to impress me after my successful robbing of the shop, Justin came round the next morning with a new plan. 'Wanna go and bust some windows?' he said.

I expressed some reservations about whether or not he was taking his reformation seriously enough.

'No problem, mate. It's cased. Cinch.'

So I concurred.

He would arrange everything of this nature in a strictly sportsmanlike manner. He had devised an elaborate scoring system that took account of distance from one's target, weight and size of missile, number of panes broken, mullions cracked and other forms of incidental damage – plants, furnishings, ornaments, plaster and so on. We were to take turns, gaining a bonus shot for every successful attempt, as in snooker.

He had taken me some way into the country to a house far from any other habitation. He explained that he had been casing the joint for some weeks now and that the owners of the house used it only at weekends. He saw it as a good target. 'They're loaded, see. They can afford it.' He was a sort of nihilistic Robin Hood; vandalising the rich to give to no one.

'So how many times have you done this before?' I asked.

'Well, you know, few times.'

'How many exactly?'

'Well, it's the first actual house I've done. I did this

greenhouse and this Portaloo on a building site. That was a right laugh. All the piss and shit went everywhere.'

'You just destroyed them, for no reason?'

'Well, yeah. For a laugh.'

'I see.'

'I've done two phone booths as well. And a windscreen. Right, you start.'

He had collected a number of missiles and stored them in a clump of rhododendrons by the roadside. He explained how each time he'd come down here he had brought one or two with him. There were bricks, pieces of concrete, a couple of old spanners, a croquet ball and some carefully rolled-up roofing lead. The first few throws produced no result, then he scored the first strike. Glass shattered in huge iceberg shapes, the sheets falling away and breaking into fragments on the garden path beneath the window. He was jumping up and down with his hands clasped above his head. His face was contorted into a grimace expressive of ecstasy. 'Bloody magic,' he said. Then signalled that we were to hide out in the bushes on the off-chance of someone having heard.

We were kneeling on the patina of moss beneath the rhododendrons.

'I have something I want you to do for me,' I said.

'Sure, anything.' He was in a state of savage excitation such as would have led him to agree to anything at that moment. My request was, in fact, rather dull.

'Well, Justin, it will seem a little uninteresting this, but I think you'll find the end result most satisfying. There's a fair deal of subtlety involved in this plan.'

'Yeah? What is it then?'

'It's very important you don't tell anyone about – '

'What d'you reckon I am? I'm your mate.'

'Of course. Right, this letter. I want you to take it and go round to my house at four tomorrow. At four exactly. It's very important you time it just right. Give it to my mother or anyone else who answers the door except – and this is essential – my father. Right? I don't expect my dad to be there at four, but just in case something goes slightly wrong. Say you found the letter lying on the ground next to where my dad normally parks his car.'

'Don't sound like no big deal to me.'
'It will be.'
'What is it then?'
'You'll see.'
'I don't get it. This letter's addressed to your dad.'
'Yes.'
'But you want me to give it to your mum?'
'Or anyone else who answers the door, except my dad.'
'So where are you gonna be?'
'Again I can't say.'
'Yeah, subtle,' he said, not without a tinge of irony.
'You'll do it?'
'Course. You're my mate.'
Then we went back to break some more windows.

11

Tenth Anniversary

1.50
Lunch was finished. Alice was seeing Angus and me off to Mrs Porter's. She was taking us into town to see an exhibition of Roman ruins.

'Goodbye, Mummy! Say goodbye to Mummy, Angus.'

'Goodbye,' Angus said.

'Be careful on the roads,' Alice warned. 'And don't forget to say thank you to Mrs Porter.'

'I won't, Mummy.'

'Good boy.'

Angus was pretending to be a funambulist along the edge of the pavement.

'Goodbye. Say goodbye again, Angus.'

'Goodbye.'

1.55
'It's a game,' I told Angus, as I trussed him to a tree in a secluded grove off the roadside. 'You're the cowboy – now, you can't argue with that, can you? – you always want to be the cowboy. You are, in fact, none other than the Lone Ranger himself, and the Red Indians have tied you up to this totem-pole.'

'But what about the – '

'Sssssh! Now, the Indians have to cut your heart out as part of an age-old ritual handed down by their ancestors. First they have to bind you fast with this rope – '

'But Mummy said we had to go straight to Mrs Porter's house.'

'That's what Mummy said. But she was wrong. And so that you can't call out for Tonto they gag you with this – '

'Bu – '

' – old stocking. Now they go off to pray to their gods before coming back to cut out your heart and eat it. Will Tonto arrive in time to rescue the Lone Ranger? Tune in next week! Same time! Same channel!'

Angus was still trying to giggle into the gag when I left him. He probably kept giggling for another minute or so and then began to get worried and wonder how long this game was going to last.

2.00

Mrs Porter's trouser-suited body appeared through the frosted glass of her front door. Her 'Big Ben' doorbell was still resonating.

'Paul!' she proclaimed. 'How nice to see you. In you come. Where's Angus? Angus is coming, isn't he?'

'I'm afraid, Mrs Porter – '

'Sandra! Will you get Peter's coat?'

'That Angus is poorly and Mummy says she's very sorry but – '

'Oh dear! Isn't that a shame? Peter! Peter! Will you leave Pinocchio's tail alone! Sandra! Have you got Peter's coat? Well go and get it then. Well, in you come, Paul.'

The house stank of fried food. It always did.

'You see the thing is, Mrs Porter, Mummy thinks – '

'Uhuh uhuh. Trrrrrr!' Peter was making gun noises.

'Be quiet! Be quiet, will you? Just for once. Paul's trying to say something.'

'Uueer! Pww.'

'That it might be mumps Angus has got, and that I might be – '

'Will you be quiet! You're not coming to the exhibition if you carry on behaving like this.'

'Muuu-um!'

' – contagious, so she thought it would be better if I didn't come.'

'Matthew! Get your coat! I don't care if you don't want it.' Peter, the youngest, was trying to clamber up the side of the Crimplene trouser suit. 'And tell Carol to come down.'

Mr and Mrs Porter were Roman Catholics. Hence the fecundity of their breeding. But this breeding programme might, feared Mr Porter, be impaired were he ever to contract the mumps. When Mrs Porter had finally taken in what I had said she was very keen indeed for me not to come to the Roman ruins. I imagine it was her intention to ring Alice just to confirm that we wouldn't be going. But that was all right: Angus had disconnected the phone again.

2.12

'Hello, Christine,' I said. She was wearing her plum-red bikini today, lying on the white tiles by the pool.

'Oh. It's you.'

'It's me.'

She was in her sultry and offhand mood, and was drying her newly painted fingernails in the sun.

'You're drying your nails.'

'Yes. I thought you were supposed to be going to see that Roman thingy with the Porters.'

'I was. I was indeed. But I thought how much more pleasing an afternoon spent with you would be.'

'Oh yeah.'

'Yes.' I walked over the tiles towards her. 'You have got brown this summer, haven't you?'

'Thanks. Paul. Paul, did you tell anyone about, you know, the other day when I let you kiss me?'

'You don't think I'd do a thing like that, do you?'

'Did you?'

'I said I wouldn't, didn't I?'

'But I want to know if you did or not.'

'I haven't told anyone yet.'

'You wouldn't?'

'Well, I don't suppose I'd have any reason to.'

'Well you'd better not. That's all.' And with that she got up and dived into the pool. She swam around under the water for a while and emerged puffing. She clambered on to the Lilo and paddled it out into the centre of the water. She was clearly angered by the ambiguity of my answers. Which was as I intended.

'I was going to tell you about *The Tempest*, wasn't I?'

'All right then.'

'The action of *The Tempest* is all set on an enchanted isle. On the isle is Prospero, the rightful Duke of Milan, usurped by – '

'What's usurped mean?'

'To wrongfully seize the throne.'

'I see.'

'Usurped by his brother Antonio. Prospero is the manipulator behind the entire course of events in the play. Unbeknown to all the other characters he is controlling everything that happens to them, but putting them into situations where they can behave in an evil way if they want, although he will stop the consequences of their evil actions affecting others.'

'Mm.'

'The storm that opens the play is summoned up by Prospero through the agency of the spirit Ariel, a magic – '

'I don't believe in magic.'

'No, but many people do.'

'Well, they're stupid.'

'All right, they're stupid. Anyway, the tempest wrecks the ship upon which are travelling Alonso, the king of Naples, his brother Sebastian, and his son Ferdinand. The wreck – '

'Is it true what you said about Mum and your dad?'

'Of course it is.'

'I thought so. I saw them this morning. Your dad came round before he went to work and they were having this argument about something. He was really angry. Do you think that means that they're not going to, you know, have their affair any more?'

Ken and Mavis's argument was of course about the letter which Mavis said she had put back in Ken's pocket – the note of Harry's which I had then removed. For the last few days Ken had been anxious to try and get a chance of talking to Mavis alone. It had not escaped my notice that he had left the house rather earlier than was usual upon this particular morning. He knew Harry was away on business.

'Well, it might do, Christine. You didn't hear what they were arguing about?'

'Well, not really.'

'We'll see.'

'I hope it does. I think it's really horrible, married people doing things like that. Do you really think they were, you know, having . . . '

'Copulating?'

'Well, yeah.'

'Yes, they were.'

'How can you be so sure?'

'I've watched them doing it.'

'You've *seen* them!'

'Yes.'

'Uueer! That's awful. Where? How did you see them . . . ?'

'They were in your mother's bedroom. I shinned up the drainpipe.'

'No!'

'Yes.'

And on it went. I spent the next half-hour or so describing in graphic detail Ken and Mavis's imaginary love-making. Christine was quite boggled by the wealth of detail I contrived. Particularly good was the description of Mavis fellating Ken while he sprawled on the dressing-table.

3.00

I walked up the garden and into the kitchen. Bananas had been farting. He always did this after having dog food with liver in it. I picked up the phone.

'Hello! Hello, Daddy, is that you?'

'Paul, what's wrong?'

'Oh, Daddy. I'm frightened. I think Mummy's being ill. She's in her room and — and the door's locked and I can't — '

'Right. Calm down. Hang on, I'm coming. Stand by the door and call out to her.'

'I have, Daddy. But she doesn't answer, she just keeps making this moaning noise. She was calling for you, I think.'

'I'm coming!' Ken declared.

'I've phoned up Mrs Edwards and she's coming.'

'Beth's coming. That's excellent. Well done. Tell her I'll be with you as soon as possible.'

'Yes, Daddy.'

And he rang off.

I went to the fridge, a new model with specially labelled compartments for vegetables, butter, eggs, cheese and canned drinks. I took the ice-cubes and pulled the little lever that released them from their tray. I prepared long cool drinks of strawberry milkshake for Christine and me, and went back to the pool.

Christine had returned to her towel on the tiles.

'I hope you don't mind,' I said, 'I just used your telephone. I had to remind Daddy that today is their wedding anniversary so he'd remember to buy a present for Mummy. He always forgets.'

'That's all right.'

I sat down on the towel next to her and put my arm round her.

'Don't,' she said, and pulled away from me. After a short period of gazing disconsolately at the surface of the pool and biting strands of her hair she said, 'I'm never going to be immoral when I'm married. I think it's disgusting.'

I endeavoured to explain that in many cultures polygamy was not only accepted, it was expected. 'Eskimos, for example,' I explained. 'For an Eskimo going to another Eskimo's igloo it is an insult if his host doesn't offer him his wife. It's like not offering someone a drink or a cup of tea in this country.'

'Well, I think Eskimos are disgusting. And anyway I think you're making that up.'

'No, honestly.'

I talked about the sexual practices of other cultures for a while. By about three-fifteen I had succeeded in persuading Christine to let me put my arm around her. She agreed on condition that I didn't 'try anything else'. There was also of course the matter of whether or not I intended telling anyone about when she let me kiss her in the field. While we did not actually discuss the matter again, it was tacitly understood that I was, in effect, blackmailing her with this possibility.

Unfortunately I had to go and make another call at this point.

3.15

I told precisely the same story to Beth. I described the terrible moaning noise Alice was making, the fact that I thought she was being sick, etc. Beth got quite worked up and promised she was coming round straight away.

I estimated that Ken was by now on the stretch of road near the pig farm. His journey home in the evenings normally took him fifty minutes, even with the special route he had devised that avoided the difficult turn. But that was during the rush-hour. I reckoned on him taking thirty-five minutes today. He would be doing about fifty, puffing ferociously on a slim panatella. I had calculated all this down to the tiniest detail.

I returned to the pool and adopted the position I had been in before leaving. Christine was still fretting over Ken and Mavis and how disgusting it all was. 'Christine,' I said, 'the world is often a cruel and confused place. I don't think you should worry about it so much. I'm sure it won't last very long. It's a bit like *The Tempest* really, if you think about it. All those people rushing round usurping thrones that belong to their brothers and so on, trying to kill each other and take control of the island. But there's a happy ending because Prospero is controlling everything. For instance, there's this evil monster called Caliban who takes up with these two drunks off the ship, and they all conspire to kill Prospero because Caliban thinks he should be the king. But in the end all the bad characters get their come-uppance and are taught that the evil of their ways does not pay.'

'But that's just a story,' she said.

'But stories are about real life.'

'Not when they're full of magic and that.'

I was by this point rubbing my hands over her tummy. I had paused to explore her pretty navel.

'Don't! It tickles!' She wriggled away. 'Anyway, how come Prospero knows what everyone's doing the whole time?'

'Well, that's very complicated to explain.'

'If you don't tell me I'm not going to let you touch my tummy any more.'

'But you like me touching your tummy.'

'Not if you don't tell me I don't.'

'I tell you what. You fetch us another drink and then I'll explain it all to you.'

'Tt,' she said, stood up and returned across the lawn with the two glasses. 'What d'you want? Banana- or strawberry-flavoured?'

'Banana, please.'

3.35

Ken's car hits the slight hillock at the top of the drive. He does not bother, as is usual, to park the car carefully so as to allow Alice to get the Vauxhall out, should she so wish, without risking damage to the paintwork on the Cortina. (Now he's been promoted he should have a Zephyr soon.) He arrives at the front door, opens it, and does not even bother to wipe his feet on the WELCOME HOME! doormat.

As Ken is rushing into the house Beth arrives at the top of the drive. She appears distraught.

Ken is on the landing and running towards the bedroom door. He calls out, and the sound of his voice wakes the sleeping Rachel who begins to cry. Under the impression that the door is in some way going to be difficult to open, he literally charges at it. In consequence of this he is flung unceremoniously into the room and trips on the end of the bed where, seconds before, Keith and Alice have suffered the discomfort of coitus interruptus. The first thing that catches Ken's eye, as he stumbles over the carpet with the stub of a cigar still clamped in his jaw, is Keith's slightly flabby stomach and its rather unusual maelstrom arrangement of hairs. Keith is kneeling on the edge of the bed trying to gather up his clothes from the floor.

Christine handed me my glass of milkshake. 'Right,' she said, 'now you've got to tell me.'

I took a long and luxuriant slurp on the milkshake, put the

glass down, and ran my hand round her waist.

'Ouw! Your hand's cold.'

Her tummy was warm.

'As I said, Prospero is a practitioner of white magic, white magic as opposed to black magic, that is. The exercising of virtuous knowledge.'

'So he is a magician?'

'It's not that simple. Prospero's magic is a discipline, a temperate and patient study of the natural world. Really, it's a little like science is today, only in Shakespeare's time they didn't have science in the way that we understand it.'

'But scientists don't know what everyone's doing the whole time.'

'That's true, but all the time science is getting closer to a fuller understanding of human behaviour that will allow – '

'But that isn't answering the question. They didn't have science in Shakespeare's time.'

I rested my hand on the bikini top.

Beth stands at the front door, uncertain whether she should enter or ring the bell even though the door is wide open. Then she can hear Ken shouting upstairs, and shortly thereafter Alice beginning to cry. Keith is remaining uncharacterstically quiet. Beth catches Ken's voice saying, 'We'll talk about this – We'll talk about this!' and then hears his great feet clumping angrily down the stairs. He rushes out into the doorway, grunts *huh!* and storms over to the car. He revs furiously and reverses back up the drive.

It's about thirty seconds before Keith, still doing up his belt (*that* belt), appears in the door before her. Beth turns white.

'Is that your thingy? Your willy?' Christine giggled. 'I didn't think boys your age did that.'

My eight-and-three quarter years' penis was indeed doing its humble best to tumefy.

'What if someone comes?'

'They won't.'

'But Mum'll be back any minute.'

'No. She's having her hair done after Andrew's dental appointment and then she's going round for tea with my mum. She won't have time to come back here.'

'How d'you know that?'

'I gave the invitation to tea myself. I was quite specific about the time.'

'All right then. But I'm not going to let you look at my tits here. You'll have to come up to the field. Just in case.'

'That's fair enough. If it will make you happy.'

'And you've got to promise never ever to tell anyone.'

'I do.'

'Promise absolutely?'

'Yes.'

4.00

My Ariel, in the very unspiritual form of Justin, arrives with his missive. It is Mavis who answers the front door and takes the letter from his hand. He delivers his spiel perfectly and departs. Alice is in the lounge crying into the cup of tea Mavis has made for her. Keith has long since departed with Beth; at least, they have left at the same time, without exactly being together.

Mavis probably takes a quick peek at the letter herself before taking it through for Alice. Either way, by the time they hear the wrenching sound of Ken's brakes on the drive, they have both read and thoroughly digested the letter's content and know the full facts about Ken's dirty weekend in Littlehampton with Sheila.

Ken enters the room with his sober and business-like expression, having resolved to discuss this thing in a calm and rational manner. His expression probably changes when he sees what document it is that Alice holds in her quivering, slightly damp hand. Quite naturally, he jumps to the conclusion that Mavis, who has been harbouring the letter all along, has just given it to Alice. Not that he can make a great display of anger on this count, in the circumstances. He would probably like to strangle Mavis for meddling in his affairs, but he does not. Instead he sits and says something to the effect of, 'I was going to tell you about that.'

Within a few minutes Mavis probably withdraws to leave the two adulterers to sort out their lives.

5.15
I have completely forgotten about Angus. The little bastard's going to make a great deal of fuss.

PART TWO

12

Angus Is Angry

Angus was as I had left him, except his eyes were pink. I decided to leave him bound and gagged while I endeavoured to explain why it was I had not come back earlier. In a desperately sympathetic tone of voice I told him how I'd meant to come straight back, but I'd just popped home to fetch a school exercise book so we (note: *we*) could take notes on the Roman ruins, when I had found Mummy was being ill. Realising that the apologetic tone of voice was quite incompatible with leaving the gag on, I decided to risk its removal.

He started screaming immediately. I covered his mouth with my hand and he bit me.

'Please, Angus, please, you've got to listen,' I implored.

He was choking on his tears and his fury. 'When I tell Mummy . . . when I tell . . . she's going to . . . going to . . . to . . . '

'Honestly, if you'll just let me explain. It was just a game. I was going to come straight back.'

'You're evil!' he screamed. 'You're evil evil evil!'

My hand was covered with his drool.

'Angus. Angus, come on, we've always been mates. I can trust you, can't I? What are mates for?'

'You'll never be my friend in a zillion trillion billion google light-years!'

'A light-year's a unit of distance. Anyway, that's not important, but just let me explain — '

'Lemme go lemme go!'

'All right. Quiet! Look, if I let you go will you promise to let me explain in a rational manner what happened? Will you?'

'No!'

'Please, Angus. We've been mates for too long for – '

'I'm going to tell Mummy and Daddy what you did and they'll know how evil you are and – and – and they'll send you away from home for ever.'

'But I can explain.'

'Mrs Porter'll say too, she'll say.'

'Look, I know it's awful what I did, I'm sorry, but if you'd just let me explain.'

'I'm going to tell. You're the most evil person in the – '

It was at this point that I lost my temper with him.

'Listen, you cringing sneaking ugly little toad.'

'Sticks and stones may break my b – '

'And they will if you don't shut up!'

'Go on! Go on! When Mummy knows wh – '

'Be quiet! Be quiet immediately!'

I had had to resort to shoving the stocking in his mouth. I left it there until he showed signs of remaining silent. 'Now, you're going to listen to what I tell you. Right?' Without removing the stocking I repeated with infinite patience the story of how I had gone home and found Alice to be ill. I liberally spiced the whole piece with apologies. It seemed to quiet him down so I took the stocking out of his mouth.

'As I say, I really am sorry, Angus. What can I do to make up for this? Is there something I can give you? Honestly, you just name it and it's yours. I mean that.'

He still wasn't saying anything.

'I tell you what, you know my Chitty Chitty Bang Bang with the wings and that. I'll give it to you. I know you like it.'

'I'm going to tell,' he said. I'd never known him so spiteful.

Then I heard a crackling in the undergrowth behind us. It was so loud it could only be the work of Ken's foot. I was petrified. I looked round and stared into the bushes. Nothing happened for a few moments. Then there was this malicious laughter and it was Justin who emerged through the foliage. He had, I gathered, been lurking there some time.

''E givin yer trouble?' he laughed.

'We're just having a minor disagreement, that's all.'

'Ang, old mate, you wouldn't put your bruvver in the shit, would you? A good bloke like you? My old mate Angus?'

He was charm itself.

It was largely through Justin's good offices that Angus was finally persuaded to go along with our story. He smiled a lot and had succeeded within ten minutes in convincing Angus that they were the best of mates. I think it was really this feeling of having discovered a friend in the world, particularly one as big and glamorous as Justin must have seemed to his child's mind, that persuaded him. I fear that alone I would never have persuaded Angus, on this occasion.

I had to have a story that would conform, approximately at least, with the facts of the afternoon that would be available to Ken and Alice or, should there be no communication between them because of the afternoon's other events, to either one of them. These facts were: my phone calls to Ken and Beth and the information they would be sure to receive from Mrs Porter. (Christine, needless to say, would not be disclosing what she knew. And if Mavis happened to mention my ringing her to invite her for tea with Alice, I could explain this as having been inspired by a desire to give Alice a pleasant surprise for her wedding anniversary. Because that part of my story was true: it was on this day that Ken and Alice were to have celebrated ten years of happy marriage.)

I had to rely on a certain vagueness about the precise timing of events. Why, for instance, was there a full hour in between my leaving Mrs Porter and my ringing Ken to tell him about Alice being ill. But I was confident that if I simply explained this time away by referring to how I had been trying to call out to Alice while she was making that terrible moaning noise in the bedroom, then she would drop the subject like a cauldron of burning fat. If this proved insufficient, I would make inquiries about who that person called Keith was. The one whose name she kept calling out. Alice most certainly wouldn't want to linger over the finer details of the afternoon. She would have to agree with me – not with Ken, he knew otherwise – that she was being sick and that I was quite right to have called Ken and Beth.

The only problem remained Angus and the account he would give of events. We untied him and Justin slapped him round the shoulders with his hand. 'Ang, old chum,' he began, 'what a laugh, aint it? You must've got really pissed off standing ere all afternoon. Anyway, what d'ya reckon on that car Paul says e's gonna give yer. You could ave his Thunderbird Two as well, wiv all the pods and that. Now, I can't say fairer than that. Look at im, will ya? He hadn't reckoned on losing is Thunderbird Two, ad e?'

And so by a sustained bout of bribery, cajolery and flattery did Justin persuade Angus to agree to our story. I had to stand there and keep smiling while Justin made Angus laugh at my expense.

We arrived home at about a quarter to six. Such was his absorption in the matter of their adultery that Ken had all this time not thought to mention the fact that it had been I who had rung him. It transpired that Alice had thought Angus and I were with Mrs Porter all along. It was Ken who answered the door.

'Is Mummy all right?' I began.

'Your mother's fine,' dour Ken said. 'And where have you been all afternoon?' Alice had appeared behind him and was reminding him that we'd been to the Roman ruins with Mrs Porter. Ken turned round and snapped at her that it was I who had phoned him at the office. She looked faintly disturbed by this revelation. So I explained what had happened.

On the way down to Mrs Porter's Angus had felt ill. I had returned home with him only to discover Alice was being ill as well. ('Yes, that's right,' Alice was only too keen to interject.) Once I had rung Ken I thought the best thing to do was to take Angus round to Justin's, because I knew that Justin's brother's girlfriend was a nurse. Justin nodded to confirm this and, encouraged by his example, Angus did the same.

Ken praised me for my initiative.

Alice ran to Angus to see what was wrong with him and said he did indeed look rather pale and his eyes were bloodshot. 'Sandra – that's my brother's girlfriend', Justin said, 'thought it was just a little tummy bug or something. Nothing to worry about.'

'That's a relief,' Ken said.

'Do you think it might have been the same thing you had, Mummy?' I asked.

'I expect it was. It must have been something we ate,' Alice said.

'You did just the right thing, well done,' Ken said, and patted me on the head. 'And well done your friend as well.'

So it was that Ken and Alice began to reappraise Justin.

Alice made tea for us, cordially inviting Justin to join us as he had been 'so helpful'. When Ken had gone through to the kitchen I hastily reconnected the telephone and it started ringing within a few seconds. Ken came back and answered it. It was Mrs Porter.

'Oh no, he's quite well now,' he was saying, 'evidently it was just a tummy bug or something. Yes. Yes I'm sure they'd love to come another day. Thank you. Goodbye.'

After tea I went out of the front door to say goodbye to Justin.

'That was pretty nifty what you done,' he said. 'You nearly cocked it up wiv Angus though.'

'Yes,' I conceded.

'D'you reckon your mum and dad'll get divorced then?'

'I don't know.'

'Well, it was pretty cool.'

'I'm glad you liked it.'

'Oh, and by the way, how far d'you go wiv that bird?'

'How did you know about that?'

'Oh, you know, I come over and ad a butcher's.'

'You did what!'

'Don't worry, mate. I had to piss off about quarter to four to bring that letter round ere. I didn't see nuffin. Well, not much.'

13

Dog's Life

Christine was a pathetic figure sitting, hunched, on a bale of straw in her welly-boots, jeans and slightly-too-tight cardigan. She was now almost permanently depressed and cried a great deal.

I would say, 'Don't cry, please,' and would brush the damp hair out of her face and wipe her salty eyes. 'Things will get better, you see if they don't.' I would put my arm round her to comfort her.

It was November and we spent a lot of time in the horse's stable, she confiding in me all her sorrows and me giving what spiritual succour I could. 'Think about something nice,' I would say. 'What do you think Tiger makes of all this crying, eh?' Tiger was the horse and, apparently, made very little of it. He would gaze with a sublime indifference from the open top of his door (we were in a small ante-room to the main stable), seemingly blind to his mistress's suffering. He snorted, and a fist of steamy breath mushroomed into the air. Then he stepped back and crapped, huge indolent dollops that steamed behind his back legs.

The riding lessons Christine was supposed to be giving me were the pretext for the many hours we spent together in the stables, though things being what they were in the house I don't imagine anyone was in the least mindful of our long absences; only Andrew, whose solitary wellies we would sometimes hear squelching across the courtyard of the stables.

'Go away!' Christine would shout.

'Why?' he'd whine.

'Because I'll tell Mummy about that picture of a nude lady you've got under the carpet in your bedroom.'

And begrudgingly would his footsteps recede.

The cause of Christine's unhappiness was the strife-torn atmosphere of their home. It had begun only days after Ken and Alice's anniversary, with arguments between Harry and Mavis, arguments that soon progressed to theatrical walk-outs, complete silences and even, on a couple of occasions, threats of violence. Christine would creep down the dark landing in her nightie and listen, horrified, to the vituperations that passed back and forth between her parents.

This turbulence had begun of course with Mavis's conviction that Ken was covering up something for Harry with his absolute denial of any knowledge of that cryptic note: 'Sorry I couldn't catch you today. Don't let Mavis know about it whatever you do. I know you wouldn't.' When Harry firmly denied ever having written such a note to Ken she was convinced. She was convinced Harry had that 'younger woman' just as Ken had Sheila. She envisaged it as a conspiracy between the two of them. She even at one point (so Christine reported to me) decided that Harry and Ken had been screwing the same girl. Harry, poor man, seriously started to think his wife was insane.

Christine had always got along better with her father than with her mother and she could not bear to hear Mavis constantly attacking Harry who, as far as she was concerned (and she was of course correct), was entirely blameless. Eventually Christine confessed to me that her sense of outrage at this had led her (as I had always purposed) to tell Harry about Mavis's affair with Ken. This really did throw petrol on things.

'I know I promised I wouldn't tell, but I just couldn't stand her always accusing him. You're not angry, are you?'

'Why should I be angry, Christine? I think you behaved in a very honourable way.'

Mavis had long since terminated any form of communication with Ken and Alice, after the day that Ken had denied any knowledge of Harry's letter. Harry, now he knew about Ken and Mavis's affair, also ceased to communicate with them. Ken had gone into the pub one evening and been amazed to see Harry walk straight out scowling. 'I don't know what's got into Harry,' he confided to me.

'I can't imagine, Daddy,' I replied.

Through the fragments of Christine's miserable lament a picture of Harry and Mavis's domestic life built up in my mind. All conversation had come to an end by about the middle of August and Harry had effectively moved into an entirely separate part of the house. He slept in the spare bedroom (but then he'd been doing that from the start), and spent his evenings and weekends in the dining-room where he had an old portable television and a single armchair he had dragged through there. The children became couriers between his territory and the living-room/kitchen area occupied by Mavis. Mavis still cooked for him but it was Christine's job to take the food through for him. There was an odd ritual of listening at doors and checking watches that ensured against unnecessary confrontations while going to the bathroom. If ever the two did happen to be in the same room at the same time they would appear not to acknowledge the existence of the other.

Gradually Christine's taking of sides with Harry became more obvious. She took to eating with him and spending most of the evening in his part of the house. Andrew was not afforded quite the same freedom of choice and remained fairly well tied to Mavis. Christine became the medium for a disjointed dialogue between the two parties: Harry would suggest, for example, that Mavis might benefit from a visit to a psychiatrist. Christine by gentle hints and illusions would convey this sentiment. And so on.

Only Bananas remained entirely neutral, equally fervent in his devotions towards both master and mistress. In consequence of this he became another weapon in the fight. 'Put the dog through there!' Mavis would tell Andrew when she tripped over his tail. Andrew would shunt the ever-willing, wildly-tail-wagging animal through into Harry's half of the house. Ten, fifteen minutes later, still wagging and still sloshing his dripping tongue round his mouth, Bananas would re-emerge with a surreptitious little push, and the dining-room door would click shut behind him.

Mavis would consign him to the garden for a while, but it was cold and wet and he scratched plaintively at the kitchen door ('I think your father ought to do something about the paint on that door'), and finally broke into a trembling wail. He would be let in, but he had done little to mitigate the dislike felt for him by Mavis; he was wet and so smelt worse than before. He would run to dry himself by the nightstore heater and the smell would intensify still more. 'That dog really is getting to be a problem,' Mavis would say. 'He isn't at all well, you know.'

Death was looming.

Death was held at bay only by the continuing silence. While Mavis and Harry were refusing to speak, they could not very well form a consensus on the subject of what to do with the dog. And the possibility of killing Bananas was the one subject for which Christine steadfastly refused to serve as messenger. Indeed, she rather cleverly put the dispute between Harry and Mavis to her advantage over this point. 'Daddy, Bananas doesn't need to be put to sleep, does he? Mummy's absolutely wrong.'

'Of course he doesn't. There's years of life in good old Bananas yet. Oh, I think he wants to spend a penny. Let him out, will you?'

At Christmas Mavis took the children to her mother's and Harry went to his parents'. Mavis returned strengthened for the fight and stopped doing Harry's laundry. Christine volunteered to do it for him but Mavis forbade it. Harry was not beaten though. He stubbornly returned every evening and took a suitcase full of clothes to the laundrette once a week. He still washed the car at weekends, but stopped doing any gardening and refused to repaint the kitchen door.

One day Mavis asked, 'Could you ask your father what he wants to do with his dog?'

'It's *our* dog!' Christine protested.

The rift deepened.

Christine began to feel she was bartering for the dog's life, with neither parent taking responsibility for it.

It was a Saturday afternoon when Harry finally left. In the morning he had made a last brave effort at sorting out their disagreements, but this had failed cataclysmically. I was just coming round for my regular riding lesson and saw Harry angrily shovelling suitcases into the boot of the car. I concealed myself among some bushes.

Mavis appeared on the threshold, dragging the reluctant Bananas by his collar. With the eerie sixth sense animals frequently seem possessed of, he knew something was wrong and dug his paws at forty-five degrees into the doormat. (This one had an art deco sunset and trees.)

'Are you intending to take your dog with you?' Mavis asked.

'*My* dog!'

She was pushing Bananas over the doormat. He yelped, then broke loose and ran across the grass towards Harry.

'What am I supposed to do with it?' Harry said. Bananas came to heel at the side of the car.

'How should I know? You should have thought of that when you got drunk and bought it off one of your drunken friends.' Mavis glowed.

'Now that is ridiculous! We bought it for the kids. You know bloody well.'

'It wasn't my idea.'

It became too much for Andrew. He came running out of the door yelling for the dog, pleading with Mavis on its behalf. He ran and knelt on the drive and wrapped his arms round Bananas's neck. In a state of powerful confusion Bananas was swivelling his head back and forth between car and house. Thick, coagulated tears in his big brown eyes.

Harry left without Bananas. Christine screamed at Mavis to leave him alone. The dog had somehow become the repository of all her love. Over the early months of spring she became quite obsessed with the dog. She moved his basket into her bedroom so as to guard him at nights, and when she went to school she locked him in the garden shed and took the key with her. '*They* can't get him while he's safe in there,' she told me.

For a while Mavis was happy with this arrangement. Christine had assumed full responsibility for the dog, even going so far as to break open her piggy-bank to buy his food and the medication he needed for his eyes. And being old, Bananas was happy to sleep most of the day and so not cause any disturbance.

'Christine,' I said, 'I don't quite know how to tell you this, but you're beginning to smell of spaniel. I think this may be having a deleterious effect on your social life.'

'Don't care!' she snapped. 'He's much nicer than people are anyway.'

'That is probably true, but none the less I should point out – '

'I don't want to know!'

And it was that, really, that signalled the end of relations between us.

When the summer came again Bananas got fleas and would yelp as he ferreted through his coat trying to catch them. Christine bought flea powder but it did very little good. The french windows being open on warm afternoons, the sound of his little yelps carried through into the house.

One evening Christine returned from school to find the lock of the shed had been sawn through. She swore she would never speak to Mavis again. Ever.

14

The Better Future

Ken and Alice's marriage teetered, passed through deathly silences, long business trips and Alice's migraines, but survived. Which was ironic in view of Mavis and Harry, neither of whom, to the best of my knowledge, had ever indulged in the slightest marital infidelity. If Ken and Alice were not exactly happier with their lives — I don't think this could ever have been the case — they did at least make every effort to appear so, to friends, to the children, to each other, even to themselves. They made great hearty displays of love and friendship, vigorously repressed what desire they might have felt to argue, and went in for lots of 'family outings' to the seaside and suchlike. Ken was for ever smiling his big clumsy grin and taking snapshots of us all. Alice became very maternal, as if to expunge the guilt she felt for the imaginary scarlet letter emblazoned on her bosom. Their rate of love-making increased drastically, as I was able to calculate from the frequency of Ken's midnight trots down the landing to dispose of their used condoms in the lavatory. (Having the things in the room overnight was one of Alice's phobias.)

I was well into my tenth year when I decided it was time to start showing a mild curiosity about some of life's mysteries. 'Mummy,' I said — she was reading the fiction section of a women's magazine — 'what does adultery mean?'

She was momentarily stuck for an answer.

'Is it something to do with adults? Like planet and planetary?'

'Well, yes, that's right, dear. It's something you'll understand when you're a bit older.' My blue eyes peered unwaveringly at her. 'It's when a married person sees someone else apart from their, er, husband or wife.'

'But you're always seeing other men apart from Daddy.'

This had the desired effect: she gasped.

'I thought it was supposed to be something that was wrong.'

'Yes, it's a bit more than just seeing them. It's to do with something men and ladies do together. You'll know about it when you're older.'

'Making babies?'

'Yes, it's to do with making babies.'

'I see.'

And Alice disappeared to tend to a saucepan in the kitchen.

It was another year or so before Ken decided it was time to have his first chat with me about the facts of life. This he did on a blustery spring day when we were in the garden looking at the newly emergent daffodils. There was a little brown patch at the bottom of the lawn from Alice's autumnal leaf-burning ritual.

'Soon, I expect,' he began, 'you'll start taking an interest in girls. Perhaps you have already? I think I was about your age when I started to get interested in girls.'

'Well, I don't think so, not really,' I said. It seemed to conform better with my increasingly intellectual image.

Throughout these few years the little girl I was most interested in was my baby sister Rachel. Where, from the first glimpse of his podgy, seemingly jaundiced face, I had felt a violent hostility towards Angus, with Rachel I was immediately besotted. I was for ever volunteering to play with her and read her stories and feed her. Alice would plonk her down on the carpet saying, 'Be careful, she's only very little,' and I would be grovelling on the carpet with rattle and plastic bricks, making baby-noises. I was the soul of gentleness, teaching her miniscule fingers to grip round mine, watching her eyes as they followed me round the room with hypnotic devotion. I loved her microscopic, perfectly formed fingernails.

As time passed she learnt to crawl, then to walk, to talk her first few baby-words, to indicate when she wanted her potty. I was particularly fascinated by her early struggles with language. I worked long hours to coax a first word from her, running through the gamut of teddy, daddy, bow-wow, mama, reading her the contents of her extensive library of Ladybird books. She was two-and-a-bit when she spoke her first definite, unambiguous word; she was alone with me, clawing at the bars of her play-pen, and she spoke: 'Da-da'. Her little hand was reaching through the bars for mine, a little sliver of drool, glistening like slug-trail, was running down her chin.

It was me she was speaking to.

I started at the grammar school. It was a pompous Victorian building, dour and ugly, the corridors and classrooms always suffused with a smell of decades-old blackened floor polish, browning, tattered textbooks and a sharp, institutional disinfectant. Dotted here and there among the grey and brown were ochre and lime-green furnishings that made weak concessions to modernity. Heavily varnished desks and tables were smeared with ink and adolescent graffiti. There were heavy, mildewed, rusting pipes and dark wooden lavatory seats.

Anachronistic in such an atmosphere was this, the concluding paragraph of one of the first textbooks given us by Dr Joseph, the science teacher. It read:

> Never have technology and science created more auspicious conditions for a better society than at this time. But whether the application of radioactive isotopes for medical purposes and the generation of atomic energy are really to be a blessing to mankind will depend, above all, on those who are now still at school. *Therefore prepare yourselves now for your work in the world of tomorrow, for it will be your world.*
> – Leonard de Vries, *The Book of the Atom*

There was a picture of statuesque man, woman and child rising like a spectre from a vast machine.

It was late afternoon in November, and Dr Joseph had lost himself again in Edenic discourse on science and the future of mankind. I glanced round the laboratory at the young generation of Dr Joseph's charges who would be inheriting this world. Sullen, gawky, pimpled faces gazed back at him, or occupied themselves with games of noughts and crosses or the exchange of petty obscenities on scraps of paper that would later be masticated into pea-shooter ammunition. These were the custodians of man's future.

Dr Joseph's desperately misguided idealism touched me with a strange poignancy. With a slow-dawning sadness I realised that he saw himself as playing his tiny role in the construction of this great and noble future: I realised that here was a rarity, a man without disingenuousness. Every day for twenty, twenty-five years he drove his low-fuel-consumption Renault and carefully parked it in the school car-park. He came in eager, fresh-faced, almost boyish in his enthusiasm, and was confronted with the drawling, slouching apathy of his pupils. He asked for no gratitude. At the end of the day he bounced down the same stairs he had come up, bearing his briefcase full of snot-encrusted exercise books on which the comic talents of the classroom had scrawled *cock* and *cunt*. He took them home and marked them with diligent, exactingly fair comments and carefully calculated percentages. He would just be crossing the asphalt — timid pigeon-steps in his vigorously polished brown, all-leather shoes, his mop of wiry yellow hair bobbing up and down — when a football would hit him in the back, coating his grey herringbone jacket with mud. 'Sorry sir! Didn't see you,' the loud, sarcastic jeer would come.

It was not to be long before Dr Joseph realised that I was rather advanced on the other pupils in the class. He came to me at the end of one lesson and sat down, resting his elbows on his knees and interlocking his pink, bony fingers. He would knead his knuckles as he spoke.

As I talked his lips disappeared into a thin, pencilled line crushed against his nose by the heavy dimple that underscored the lower lip. 'Mmm,' he said, 'I hadn't realised you had done any science at the primary level.'

'I didn't, sir. But I've tried to teach myself a bit.'

'Well, remarkable! Your father taught you a little perhaps?'

'I'm afraid not, sir. My father isn't really very interested in science.'

'No one has helped you at all?'

'Well, not really, sir.'

'Well, I must say, you seem remarkably knowledgeable.'

'Thank you, sir.'

It was clear that Dr Joseph and I were made for one another. He was shifting around on his chair so that the legs grated over the polished floor as he spoke. I told him how I had never had anyone I could ask questions of, or discuss the results of experiments with. He was so happy after all these years to have discovered this one brilliant and enthusiastic pupil. I portrayed myself as a lonely child, dedicated to the acquisition of knowledge and, until now, never having received any encouragement. His face filled with a supernal bliss.

'And what sort of thing have you done?' he asked.

'Well, sir . . . ' I was portraying myself as he seemed to want me — quiet, withdrawn, rather timid. 'I'm particularly interested in animal biology . . . ' (This was his area of specialisation.)

'Uh-huh,' he said, his head nodding very gently.

'I have constructed a wormery with different layers of soil, er — chalky, clay, loamy, gravelly, er, so as to observe the way in which the worms' burrowing mixes the soils together . . . ' (His doctorate thesis had been on the earthworm.)

'Well, that's fascinating. The worm is of particular interest to me, in fact. Tell me what else you've done.'

We went on to discuss many of his pet subjects. He told me how he was involved in the campaign against vivisection and I told him that I was a junior member of the RSPCA. We discussed the evils of battery farming and the near extinction of many species of animal. I delivered myself of a precocious and sanctimonious homily about science being in danger of ignoring many of the creatures we shared the earth with in its endeavours to better the lives of people. It was, in fact, no more than a précis of many remarks he had made during the previous months on exactly this subject.

There were almost tears in his eyes by the time I had finished.

It was after a few more sessions like this that Dr Joseph decided to see what he could do about having me put forward a couple of years in the science curriculum. He was convinced that my talents were being wasted.

He was standing in his grubby lab-coat, streaks of ink and acid burns visible down its back as he turned and walked towards the window. There was a paper pellet trapped in his hair. 'Don't hold out too much hope,' he told me. 'The Head of Science isn't very keen on putting pupils forward in this way.'

'I appreciate your efforts on my behalf, sir.'

'Well, we can't stifle talent, can we? I'll speak to the Head of Science tomorrow.'

'Thank you, sir.'

15

King Brown

It was during my first year at the school that I began to build up my first laboratory. I could not be a scientist without a proper laboratory to call my own. It was located in an old shed at the bottom of Justin's garden, a setting practical for a number of reasons: it was furnished with a large array of tools and two sturdy benches, equipped with vices, that could be put to the purpose of building the equipment that was necessary for my work. It was well soundproofed. There was a power supply, wired from the house many years before in the days when Mr Burrows used it. And it was right at the bottom of the long, thin, wildly overgrown garden, a good distance from the nearest house, and well-masked with trees and the unkempt creepers that sprawled over decaying trellises.

No one ever went to it.

Justin's mother had died two years before, leaving the elderly father, and two brothers and a sister, all older than Justin. He was, I always presumed, by way of a late, unexpected arrival. Sean, the eldest brother, was a private in the army and rarely came home; Chris, the second, had married when he was seventeen and emigrated to Canada for 'a new life'. The new life was advertised in a brochure depicting lakes set between soaring mountains thick with firs, and green, undulant golf courses. A family drove in a white convertible. White teeth shone out of their bronzed faces. They said, 'We have a lot of money.'

Chris took a job cutting down some of the trees that frilled the mountains (planetary defoliation), bought a house in a suburb and gave Justin a nephew and a niece, called Mick and Bianca. Echoing the words of the brochure, Chris wrote to Justin on his birthday urging him to come over when he left school. 'It's a place where you can be yourself,' he wrote. Justin was giving it serious consideration.

Only Justin's sister remained at home, looking after Mr Burrows. He came in from work and shouted up the stairs at her for his tea, 'Girl! Where are ya, girl?' I was happy to discover that 'girl' was his way of pronouncing her name, Gail.

Mr Burrows was a mechanic at the local garage. He had at one point set up his own business, but it had collapsed on account of his stupendous and lofty lack of business acumen and his penchant for absurd schemes. Gail would make tea and toast, and Mr Burrows would regale Justin and me with accounts of his short-lived business, and the hard-earned pearls of his personal philosophy. He would describe one of his more ludicrous projects, a revolutionary coal-powered racing car, for instance, and then wait with menacing facial grimace to see whether or not we laughed. Generally we *were* supposed to.

It was as a result of his collapsed business that the shed was so well-stocked. There was welding equipment, an hydraulic pump, an electric saw, a vast reserve of old, black, oil-caked engines in various stages of deconstruction, a lathe and an elaborate cage-like structure that had once served as Mr Burrows's private office. To this I gradually added: a collection of chemicals, glassware, bunsen-burners, microscope, library of reference books, experimental animals (mice, locusts, rabbits), bacterial cultures, voltmeter, syringes, bell-jars, scalpels, needles, surgical scissors and so forth.

Because of what I considered to be the implacably paternalistic nature of society I had been driven to stealing most of these things from the school. Later I was to acquire some goods from a West Indian boy called Winston whose big brother robbed chemists.

Stealing with Justin was always a theatrical event. He would assume different roles for different 'jobs'. We stole sulphuric acid together and he was Buster Edwards; locusts and we – so he would have it – were the Kray twins. He specialised in breaking and entering and what he termed 'communications'. These normally took the form of an elaborate system of animal noises he had worked out. I had objected to this. 'But Justin, the whole point of using animal noises is if you are in the wild, where there *are* animal noises,' but I don't think he ever fully grasped this point.

'But I'm good at animal noises,' he said.

The Head of Science, an intermittent and rather eccentric collector of rare species, had recently acquired two king brown snakes which he displayed for the edification of select pupils in his personal office. I had gone in to see him in connection with my studies. At Dr Joseph's instigation I had now been put forward two years in the science curriculum, and was in addition receiving private tuition from both Dr Joseph and the Head of Science. My rise had been rapid and it was now being mooted that I might soon be ready to take my science O levels, three years ahead of the normal timetable. I went into the office and began immediately to ask enthusiastic questions, and at the same time demonstrate my considerable knowledge on the subject of snakes. The Head of Science was both impressed and flattered, and proceeded to tell me how he was expecting the mother to start laying her eggs within the next couple of days. What ecstasy boiled within me!

I sought permission for Justin and myself to watch the female while she was laying her eggs. The Head of Science was picking lumps of nicotine-encrusted hair from his nostrils, unabashedly rolling it into tight little balls that he dropped in the ashtray. He relished this kind of delaying tactic: he liked to see my bright and eager face hanging on his next word, on his authority.

'Justin Burrows? Do I know him?'

'Yes, sir. He's in the second year, in class three.'

'A friend of yours?'

'Yes, sir.'

'Mmmm.' He was now starting that ponderous process of packing another pipe full of St Bruno. My eyes were dragged round to the caged, glass cabinet where the snakes slept, recently fed. They were divided by a glass partition, necessary, the Head of Science had told me, because of the male's recent inclination to attack the female. 'Even though she's pregnant?' I had asked. 'Paul, Paul,' he had replied, 'something you will learn: the snake is an unpredictable creature. Sometimes mild, sometimes brutal, irrational.' And his eyes leered at me from under the thick umbrellas of eyebrow.

'You understand that the snakes are not really for the perusal . . . ' (after a slightly unusual use of vocabulary he would stop, as if to measure its effect) ' . . . of the younger pupils. For you of course I can make an exception, but for your friend – what was his name?'

'Justin Burrows, sir.'

'Yes. I don't think I can grant permission there.'

I waited while he lit the pipe, billows of smoke rising up around him, then blew out the small glimmer of flame that remained at the base of the blackened, curved England's Glory match.

'Well, sir, I think – '

'It would set a precedent, you understand. *Everyone* would want to see the snakes, and – how shall I put it? – for not altogether scientific reasons. Mm.' His eyebrows moved up.

'I quite understand that, sir. I think however that in this particular case there might be good reason for making an exception. Justin – '

'But where would the exceptions stop? Eh? First there is one exception. Then there is another. And another. And another. You take my point?'

The Head of Science had a penchant for dialectical debate. He had that trait of all inadequate intellectuals who have become schoolteachers that they might puff out their slight talents with the authority of their position, and the youth of their interlocutors. That they might imitate the sort of dialogues they imagine take place in the senior common rooms of Oxford and Cambridge, in the private studies of research institutes. (Unlike Dr Joseph, the Head of Science's professional motivations were quite clear to me.)

The Head of Science particularly enjoyed playing this game with me because I put up a good fight but always allowed him to win in the end. This he usually did by having recourse to some recondite volume he presumed (sometimes correctly) I had not read. He would say, 'Ah, experience. Age, sir. I recommend you read that at some point. A thought-provoking work, certainly,' nodding. Nodding lethargically. On other occasions he would make reference to his own single published work, a now outdated general guide to botany. I had of course read it and committed a considerable quantity of its frankly dreary text to memory. I was thus in a position to both flatter and impress him again. 'Yes, sir. But then do you not say in, Chapter Seven, I think it is, of your book, that the ecology of the duck-pond is dependent upon the water snail?'

I cannot tell you how deeply this titillated his pathetic vanity.

On this occasion however I could not allow him to win the argument. I needed Justin's assistance to steal the snakes' eggs.

'The exceptions stop, sir,' (heavy Boswell-and-Johnson inflexion), 'where you say they do. It is surely a matter for your judgment, dictated by your authority.'

Thoughtful silence. 'You are certainly turning into an impressive debater, Paul.' He sucked on his pipe and I heard the little globules of spittle that gathered in its tube. 'On this occasion I will let your friend see the snakes. Provided you can find a member of staff who will be prepared to supervise your visit after school hours. Is that fair?'

'Yes, sir. Thank you.'

Miss Colley was the teacher I had selected for this purpose. She was young, just out of university, a trusting, charitable girl with a naive, unsullied dedication to the ideals of education. She was attractive, with largish breasts Justin described as bouncing like those of an Olympic runner.

She was marking her exercise books, Justin and I watching the female snake in suitably awed silence. There was a slight, tremulous contraction that seemed to indicate the delivery of another egg. Justin was trying to outstare the male, angered by the fact that snakes did not seem to respond as well to his brutal expression as people did.

'Can I go to the lavatory, Miss, please?' he said.

'Of course you can. It's not a lesson now, you know,' she laughed. Miss Colley was of that class of schoolteachers stupid enough to imagine that it was a good idea to try and treat her pupils as equals. A few years' brutal experience would, I was sure, persuade her of the folly of this notion.

'Thank you very much, Miss.' (How well I had trained him.)

I remained by the cabinet, fixated by the snakes' eyes, beguiled by their twisting, smooth bodies. The mother's body spiralled around the eggs, like chocolate drops. Leathery balls of chocolate.

'You're not frightened at all of snakes then?' Miss Colley asked. I turned to look at her.

'No, Miss. No, I don't understand why people are so afraid of snakes. Unprovoked, they are perfectly harmless to man. It is an entirely irrational fear.'

'Yes! It certainly is that.' Her exclamation masked a certain nervousness. Something steely in my words. 'But one can't always be entirely rational, can one? I must say they still send a bit of a shiver down my spine, even knowing they're safely locked away.'

'Oh, I can understand that, Miss. Don't you feel however that one of the jobs of science is to help us overcome that sort of irrational fear?'

'Well, let's hope so.'

'I mean it is irrational fear of that sort that is behind so many of man's worst actions. It is irrational fear of black people that motivates racial hatred, for example.'

'Yes, that's a very interesting point, Paul.'

(Sometimes, reflecting on this, I wonder why it was no one ever just turned round and said, 'Why don't you shut up, you precocious brat?' I would have done.)

'Miss, do you think there is any truth in Freud's ideas about snakes?'

For a moment it appeared she had not properly taken in my question. Or perhaps her mind was scanning itself for a trace of her undergraduate essay on phallic symbols. 'Well,' she said, a touch nonplussed I thought, 'I'm surprised you have read Freud.'

'Yes, Miss. *The Interpretation of Dreams*, *The Three Essays on Sexuality*, and a few other things.' The opening of a short piece from 1913, 'Two Lies Told by Children', passed through my thoughts: *We can understand children telling lies, when in doing so, they are imitating the lies told by grown-up people.* I had long thought of this as a gloriously ironic justification for many of my actions. Kind-hearted Sigmund goes on to describe another category of lie *told by well-brought-up children: These lies*, he tells us, *occur under the influence of excessive feelings of love*.

I would have to beg to differ there.

'Well, I think you must know more about Freud than I do,' Miss Colley said. Another mistake the schoolteacher should never make: admitting the pupil's superior intellect.

Then I began, 'But would you think Freud was correct in seeing the snake as a symbol of the male organ of sex?' but was cut off on the last few words by Justin's scream.

'What's happening?' Miss Colley gasped, leaping up, spilling her exercise books on to the floor, and rushing towards the door. As she ran through the laboratory her heels echoed around its tall, cold walls. Then came a second scream from Justin, a reinforcement just in case the first had failed to communicate itself. It was a hideous noise.

I went to the door, took the latch off, and closed it with a clean, voiceless click. The key remained safely in Miss Colley's handbag, inside the locked room. I was a prisoner.

I found the keys to the cage that surrounded the snakes' glass cabinet. They were where I had expected to find them in the Head of Science's drawers, along with some of the fruits of his obsessive collecting of things: neat rows of England's Glory matchboxes he stored dead insects in, shells, pebbles, fossils, and children's model soldiers of the Eighth Army. *Since then*, says Sigmund again, *there has been a general consensus of opinion that each of the three qualities, avarice, pedantry and obstinacy, springs from anal-erotic sources – or, to express it more cautiously and more completely – draws powerful contributions from those sources*.

The Head of Science was an anal character.

I took note also of a pair of pearl-inlaid opera glasses.

Having unlocked the cage I slid back the cover of the cabinet a couple of inches and the two heads followed me like bendy-rubber stereoscopic periscopes. I felt a spurt of something hot and acidic deep in my stomach, and tried hard to concentrate my mind on something pleasant. This was not very easy. I imagined placing one of my fully grown king browns in the tub of Alice's front-loader, imagined her hand reaching in and momentarily mistaking him for one of the grey hoses that had to be affixed to the taps. I saw her bending over to chat with one of the garden gnomes, and king brown's malice-oozing grin sneaking out from behind Benjy's bell-topped hat. I came walking down the garden, stepped over her paralysed body and called him, as one would call a faithful labrador: 'Come on boy! Good boy!' He bounded out from the rockery and dashed over to me, coming to heel to beg for his dinner: Angus's hamster. He performed a trick, balancing a tennis ball on his forehead. 'Good boy!' Alice's screaming was pitched beyond audibility, reminiscent of a dog whistle. A wild baying of neighbourhood dogs starts up.

I stabbed the Head of Science's cane (rarely used, but used with neat, precise, well-calculated blows when it was) against the neck of the female, pinning her against the glass with such vigour I thought I had ruptured her skin. On the other side of the glass partition the male lurched up and glared at me. I could feel the sweat stinging in my armpits.

'Paul! Paul? Are you in there?' Miss Colley was banging on the door. My pursed lips remained silent. 'Paul! Are you all right?'

'It's all right, Miss.' Justin had come up behind her. 'He must have gone to catch the bus. He's probably waiting down in the car-park. Shall I go and look?'

'Yes, do that.' Justin's heavy, ungainly step receded back through the laboratory. The female was flailing her tail, but I had now cupped the first egg with the Head of Science's six iron, and was sliding it gently up the glass, less than an inch from Daddy's indignant grin.

I heard Miss Colley let out an exasperated whimper, bang her heel on the floor in an atavistic display of frustration, then walk briskly away. Her delicate tapping contrasted pleasingly with Justin's stomp. The first egg flopped gracefully into the cotton-wool-lined beaker taped to the side of the display case: I felt a craftsmanlike satisfaction. Miss Colley had gone to look for the school caretaker so as to get the duplicate key to the door. Were she to return prematurely Justin would re-enact the attack of cramp with which he had got her to massage his leg on the floor of the lavatories. In between his cries of pain he would assure her that he had seen me downstairs, thus lessening the urgency of her return to the office.

The fangs snapped together as I released the cane, but she did not attempt to attack me. I packed the two eggs in my pencil-case with enormous care, wrapping them in cotton-wool, then returned the room to its former state, even taking the time thoughtfully to gather up the exercise books Miss Colley had dropped when she left. As I was leaving by the ladder Justin had placed beneath the window – 'vertical descent' – I noticed that the female was laying another egg, already covering my tracks.

My snake-breeding programme was under way.

16

The Prodigy

I had taken five O levels – Physics, Chemistry, Biology, Mathematics and Additional Mathematics – attaining a grade one pass in every one. I was just thirteen. I became, temporarily, a kind of public property.

I was photographed for the local newspaper bearing in my hands the certificates of my achievement and, as was thought appropriate by the editor, a test-tube as emblem of my craft. I looked like a scientist in one of Dr Joseph's books, only an infantile parody. With my John F. Kennedy hairstyle and smile I was some kind of omen for the future: the child prodigy, the scientific Mozart. The headline over my picture: EINSTEIN OF TOMORROW?

Alice was almost overwhelmed by the notoriety my successes brought to the family. She redoubled her efforts to impress upon Angus that he was *not* stupid. She told him he was the artistic one, and so began Angus's career as a painter. I confronted him with his new-found vocation.

'I hear you have aspirations towards being an artist, Angus. Do let me see some of your paintings, I'd be very interested.'

He had gone brilliant red: vermilion.

Alice came in. 'Perhaps Angus isn't – perhaps Angus doesn't want to show you any of his pictures yet.'

'I do apologise, Angus. Excuse my over-zealous enthusiasm to see your work. But of course, if you're going to make a living as an artist, you'll have to be prepared to show your work sooner or later. I assume it is your intended career.'

On another occasion I came across him with his paintbox on the patio. He had been trying to get some painting in while I was out. 'Ah! You are eschewing figurative art altogether then, Angus?' He tried to snatch the watercolour pad out of my hands. 'A whole-hearted embrace of abstraction, eh?' In his desperation he had knocked the paintbox off the table.

'Piss off, Paul!'

'Ah-ha. That volatile artist's temperament displaying itself already.' I smiled at him.

'Leave me alone! Piss off!'

'Many of the great artists have lived lives of torment, Angus. It is the price that has to be paid for artistic greatness. Beethoven and Michelangelo, Milton's blindness. But I'm sure you know all about that from the Time-Life book about Van Gogh that Mummy has got for you from that book club.'

'Leave me alone!' He was crying.

'I detect the influence of Cubism here. I'm not sure you've proportioned this figure quite correctly, but perhaps that was not your intention. The relationship between Cubist theory — the giving of many perspectives at once — and the theory of relativity is a very interesting one. We must discuss it some time.' I was holding his picture of a man standing in front of a river. A huge slab of dirty brown with a pink face on top of it and a thick streak of blue behind it. He was running inside the house, screaming.

'Ah! Kirk Douglas in *Lust for Life*,' I called after him. (Alice was out shopping.)

Ken too was a little bemused about how he should react to my prodigious academic performance. I began to detect in him a sense of jealousy. His almost puritan devotion to the work-ethic made him feel that there was something rather unnatural in my apparently effortless success. Because I was his son his feelings were obviously contradictory: at once he was beginning to envy me, to perceive me as in some sense a rival (I had read all about feelings of male inadequacy in the recently published *The Female Eunuch*), but at the same time I was the fruit of his seed, an extension of him.

Perhaps to compensate, or disguise these feelings, Ken magnanimously declared that he was going to buy me a special p esent by way of congratulation. He appeared home one evening proudly bearing the Junior Scientist Microscope Kit. I, of course, already possessed a superior microscope in my secret laboratory.

'Thanks very much, Dad. It looks really good.'

Proudly, happily, with his dominance firmly re-established by his deed of gift-bearing (there's nothing like an act of charity to make people feel good about themselves), he replied, 'That's all right, Paul. I didn't pay through the nose for it, of course.' Of course he hadn't: he had got it cost-price from a client. This made the achievement all the greater.

'It's so good.'

'You've earnt it. Well done.'

The microscope had to go on proud display in the bedroom I shared with Angus and be brought out when visitors called and the inevitable subject of my academic achievements came up. Ken would look at me with his serious expression and say discreetly, 'Go and fetch the microscope, Paul, and show it to Linda and Ted.' He was marketing me.

Dutifully smiling, I walked through to the bedroom and returned carefully cradling the cheap microscope. I placed it on the coffee table in a space the gleeful Linda had cleared between the Danish-style ashtray (marble with copper Copenhagen mermaid) and the Remy Martin bottle.

'This is a sample of algae gathered from a pond.'

Linda cocked her eye to fit it over the microscope. The smell of the hairdresser's was still keen in her hair.

'And this one is the nasturtium leaf. Would you like to see a human hair magnified?'

'How fascinating!'

'That's really quite something!' Ted weighed in. I could smell his nylon shirt and its day's office-sweat. His mouth smelt of slim panatella and brandy, which mingled in the air with Linda's Oil of Ulay and St Moritz cigarettes.

'This is a cross-section of a worm, Linda. Shall I show you?'

I showed her.

'This one is a – be careful there, Ted. If you open the iris diaphragm too wide you'll find that it impairs the definition. A human toenail cutting.'

'Fascinating! Have you seen this, Linda?'

They'd always giggle over the toenail cutting. I could never see why they found it so funny. Everyone I ever showed the magnified toenail cutting to felt it was mandatory to find it amusing. And always Ted and Linda – there were hordes of Teds and Lindas – would return home and buy microscopes for their progeny. They wanted them to be as brilliant as me.

Ken and Alice had been on a couple of occasions to visit the Head of Science in his mouse- and algae-smelling office. He had described me as a prodigy and forcefully asserted that every possible encouragement, facility and opportunity should be afforded me. This I suspect was occasioned by the concern Dr Joseph had expressed to him that I was not receiving enough parental motivation, which in turn had been occasioned by the portrait of myself I had offered Dr Joseph. And it was the Head of Science's words that were responsible for precipitating the pathetic spectacle of Ken purchasing *A Layman's Guide to Modern Science* so as to equip himself for conversations with his prodigious son. After an early dinner he would light a slim panatella and we would retire out to the patio for a man-to-man talk about science.

It was a warm summer evening. One could hear the dim clatter of plates as Alice washed up, the drone of music from the television Angus sat goggling at. He was watching *Star Trek*, his favourite programme. Ken offered me a small glass of well-watered Johnnie Walker. 'Thanks, Dad,' I said. We talked in short, clipped lines as befitted the calm of the evening. Ken cupped his blue chin in his palm for a while and surveyed his domain: the neat, semi-landscaped garden with the row of Christmas trees, the rockery, the rose-bed, the gnomes. Though he rarely said so, he did not much care for the gnomes. One of Alice's sillier ideas. But since that time, the time he and Sheila, Alice and Keith . . . he tried to avoid arguments – plumped for a quiet life. He no longer made sharp comments about the dried flower arrangements clogging up the house (though Alice made far fewer these days), and when the subject of money came up he was calmer, more circumspect. 'We'll see,' he said, and Alice nodded. She seemed happier to respect his decisions.

After a while he weighed in with his first inanity gleaned from the *Layman's Guide*.

'That's a very interesting point, Dad. I think there probably will be some kind of space settlement by the end of the century, perhaps sooner. It's difficult to say.'

I felt as though there were lead weights attached to my brain.

'Do you think the Russians will do it?' he asked. Ken imagined that the Russians were still desperately concerned about getting to the moon. With crystal clarity I could remember 20th July 1969, and the extraordinary kind of patriotism that filled Ken as we sat round the TV watching the moon landing. We. The West. Mankind. We'd done it. Ken was momentarily filled with Dr Joseph-style idealism.

'Do what, Dad?'

'Get to the moon.'

'I don't think they're very concerned about getting to the moon any more.'

'Oh.' He cupped his chin again.

Other evenings Justin came over and kicked a ball about with Angus. He seemed to find it much easier to be nice to Angus than I did. I always wanted to hurt Angus, but my treatment of him was still conditioned by the possibility that he could yet tell Ken and Alice what I had done to him all those years ago. When I felt a real need to punish him I had to get Justin to do it. He worshipped Justin the way Norman worshipped me. Similarly when I had tormented Angus by passing critical judgment on his paintings I would have to get Justin round to be nice to him. It caused me untold pain to see his ugly little face lighting up with joy when Justin deigned to play football with him. When this pain became unbearable I would have to take Justin aside and ask him to injure Angus.

'Nobby Stiles?' he'd ask, 'or Hacker Hunter?' Justin was an expert on the different defensive techniques of association football.

'I don't mind. Just hurt him.'

'All right. Keep yer hair on.' And he ran stealthily across the lawn, glancing round to see if Alice was at the kitchen window. 'Right, Angus!' he called, 'I'm in goal. You try and score.'

Angus would immediately start adopting postures he took to resemble those of professional players. He'd point his arms out like a short chubby ballerina and dribble the ball round imaginary defenders. Sometimes he would hurl himself down on the grass as though he had been tripped by one of these, and his squeaky little voice would demand a penalty from the referee. My flesh would quake with loathing and contempt. 'Is Angus hurt?' Rachel would say.

'No, Angus is just pretending he's been fouled. There's a big difference between a pretend foul and a real one. Justin's going to show us what a real foul looks like.'

It was at this point that Justin came charging out of the goal-mouth. Angus tried to shoot but it was too late. Justin had felled him. He lay clutching his little fat leg.

'Is Angus hurt now?' she said.

'I think so.'

Justin was standing over him. 'You all right? Was a bit rough. Sorry, mate.'

Angus would cry for five minutes, then forgive him.

17

Norman the Cyberman

It was snowing outside, the snow piling up in thick ridges against the pieces of old engine, masking and blurring the brambles and the husks of the creepers that trailed up the rotten trellises. The snow rendered the sharpest forms into big, blubbery Henry Moore sculptures. A light fall, fine and dusty, glowed with the yellow light that emanated from the back room, where Mr Burrows sat in his slippers with the gas fire misting up the windows and *Grandstand* blasting from the TV in dispute with his deafness. He was probably dozing, waiting for the half-time results. Gail was out shopping in the town, stopping to watch Father Christmas in the window of Debenhams as he distributed gifts from the pixie grotto into the grabbing hands of overweight children with dribbling noses and chocolate smeared round their greedy little mouths. It was a truly Dickensian Christmas.

Inside the lab Norman was seated in a red leather car seat with specially attached arm-rests that had been welded on by Justin. His wrists were strapped to the arm-rests. I had told Justin I doubted the strapping was necessary, but he would have it this way. He always desired the sensational result. 'Science is subtler than that,' I told him, 'more complex in its manifestations.'

'Yeah, course,' he grunted.

He was the same with every experiment we performed. When we crossbred worms, for instance, he hoped for some mutant superworm that would attack blackbirds. I had asked him what the point of this would be.

'Be a good laugh, like,' he'd answered.

I would feel angered by the irksome simplicity of his motivations. 'I am a scientist!' I'd say. 'I am exploring the contours of the natural world.'

'Yeah, right.'

'So leave the decision-making to me, will you?'

He would always mumble apologetically and plunge himself into something that would prove his usefulness to me.

On this occasion it had been into the construction of the leather straps that were to bind Norman's ankles. Justin had stolen an old motorcycling jacket from his father and converted it. He had also contrived a three-inch steel band, padded with foam rubber, that secured Norman's waist to the car seat. While he did this I occupied myself with the theoretical side of the project. I read to him the relevant passages from the seminal work, Cannon's *Bodily Changes in Pain, Hunger, Fear and Rage*, the last-named of these conditions being that which we were endeavouring to induce in the normally passive Norman.

Justin was returning through the snow, wiping his nose on the back of his hand, jogging up and down to keep warm. It was warm in the lab from the electric fires that dangled over the converted aquarium in which the king browns lived. I walked over to look at them. 'We're going to build a greenhouse outside for you,' I said, 'in the summer. Isn't that right, Norman?'

'Yeah,' his muffled voice came from the car seat.

Justin came bursting in through the door, a sharp squall of cold following him. 'This be all right?' he asked, holding up a piece of asbestos brake-liner.

'It looks okay. Try it.'

He went over to Norman and lifted off the elaborate apparatus that enveloped Norman's skull. He tried the asbestos inside it and nodded to indicate he thought it was right. He pushed it back down over Norman's head. 'Tight enough, Norm?' he asked.

Norman grunted.

'You all right, Norm?' I asked. 'Want another Digestive Cream?'

'Er, no, er like . . . I'm not really hungry.'

'Fair enough. Just thought I'd ask. Anything else you want? Let's have another little check-up, shall we?'

I picked up my stethoscope.

'What you doin?' Justin said.

'I am conducting an auscultation of Norman's borborygmi.' (Justin was irritating me.) 'Norman, you're not still nervous, are you? I thought we'd been through all that.'

'No, I, er – '

'It's because of the electricity, isn't it? Now, we've discussed this at great length, haven't we? Electricity is a good thing, nothing to be frightened of. It does nice things like heat people's baths and run their TVs, so there's really nothing to be afraid of. Have another biscuit.' I shoved a Digestive Cream into his mouth.

'Ave a bernaarner!' Justin sang. 'You're all right, aren't yer Norm?'

'Don't take the mickey out of Norman, Justin. He might think you're being serious.'

'You wouldn't think that, wouldja, Norm? Course he wouldn't. Good fit that elmet, aint it?' he went on, patting the head apparatus with increasing vigour. He was like an overexcited dog wagging its tail too fast.

'That'll do, Justin. Let's get on. Can you attach the electrodes and the moisture detector, please?'

'Right.' He busied himself with the various gadgets that were to run off Norman's anatomy. Bits of wiring, tubing and so forth; a stethoscope attached to Norman's abdomen and running into a cassette recorder that would measure the amount of stomach movement. Norman looked increasingly perturbed. 'Right, that's it.' Justin snuffled on to his sleeve.

'Wipe your nose properly, Justin. Then we can get on.'

'Sorry.' And he started searching round the lab for something to blow his nose on. He came across Norman's raincoat hanging on the back of the door.

'Don't!'

'What's wrong?'

'Justin, the whole point of this experiment is to artificially stimulate Norman's aggressive faculty. If you wipe your nose on his raincoat he's going to get angry anyway, so the experiment will be a waste of time.' This whole issue had long been one Justin failed fully to comprehend. He could see no point in artificially rousing Norman to aggression by the electrical stimulation of his hypothalamus if the same result could be arrived at simply by, for instance, blowing his nose on Norman's raincoat.

'But he don't mind, do ya, Norm?'

'No, er – ' shaking the metal-clad head.

'Norman may not appear to mind. That is not the relevant consideration. He may not even *know* that he minds. The human brain is an enormously sophisticated and sensitive instrument. Blow your nose on something else.'

'All right. Stone the crows.' He looked round the lab and alighted upon another suitable receptacle for his mucus. Again I had to forestall him.

'No. What's wrong with using that, Justin?'

'Dunno. Looks all right to me.'

'Think about it.'

He thought about it. Norman's face indicated that he at least had worked out what was wrong.

'Ask Norman. He knows.'

'All right then. Norm, why shouldn't I blow my nose on this?'

'Er, like, because that's the gag that you've got to put round my mouth in case I make a noise during the er, experiment like.'

'Oh, right. Sorry about that, mate.'

Finally, when Justin had blown his nose and Norman had been gagged, we were ready to begin. The lights were turned off and a theatrical hush fell over the lab. The only light came from the glowing bars of the electric fires and the grey and mossy window.

I spoke quietly. 'Now, there is nothing to hurry us, nothing to disturb us. When the day's experiment is finished we'll all go and have tea with Justin's dad and have the remainder of the day off. So let's all do our best. Justin, start at ten volts.'

The switch clicked and a small green disc lit up on the control panel. A gentle purring noise filled the room. We waited thirty seconds or so, and my mind filled up with the glorious possibilities of what I was now doing. I envisaged

Norman rising from the car seat like a wild animal. But when I told Justin to switch off the voltage nothing seemed to have happened. I inspected the monitoring devices and found only a slight increase in the flow of digestive juices. Norman was entirely motionless.

'Try again. Fifteen volts.'

I left the current on longer this time and occupied myself with feeding a can of pilchards to the snakes. Their two bodies coiled around one another as they vied for my attention, snapping and hissing to demand the fillets of fish. I would become quite affectionate when feeding my snakes.

'Switch off.'

Justin remained gazing at the trussed figure of Norman.

'Off!'

He snapped to attention and turned off the apparatus.

'Remove the gag. Carefully, he might be violent.'

'Yeah?' A note of relish in his voice. He smacked his lips at the prospect of having forcibly to resist the raging animal Norman would have become.

'Justin, you are not to hurt Norman at any cost. Understand?'

'Well, yeah. But I mean what if he – '

'You'll have to let him hit you. If the experiment has worked we will have to let him work it out of his system.'

'But like what – '

'No questions.'

'You never said nothin about him being allowed to hit me before.'

'Never mind. Get on with it.'

Hurriedly he undid the gag, his clumsy, stumpy fingers having trouble with the knot he had tied so thoroughly. When it came off he stepped back with a little hop.

Nothing.

'Remove the head apparatus.'

'You reckon he's all right?' (Amazingly there seemed to be a note of genuine concern in his voice.)

'Head apparatus. He'll be fine.'

Cautiously he began to unscrew the bolts that secured the sides of the helmet to Norman's temples. The coloured wires that ran from the helmet shook as he worked.

Norman's hair was ruffled, poking out in odd spike-shapes. His eyes were clamped shut and his mouth dangled open once the gag came off.

'You don't reckon e's bitten the dust, do ya?' Justin asked.

'Of course he hasn't. Norm? Are you awake, Norm?'

'I don't reckon he's breathing.'

'Of course he's breathing. Give him a light slap round the face.'

Justin slapped him and a pink glow returned into his cheek. I went over and lifted his eyelids. The eyes were like those of a waxwork.

'His mum'll be really pissed off if he's dead.'

'Shut up!'

'Sorry.'

'He's in some kind of trance, that's all. Sort of suspended animation.'

'The living dead like?'

'Again you hyperbolise. Give him another slap.'

Justin did this and Norman stirred. He snorted violently a couple of times and then groaned something. Suddenly he jolted up in the seat, his eyes wide open. Justin leapt back. Norman said something about the jungle then collapsed back into somnolence.

'He nearly made me shit myself,' Justin said.

We left Norman asleep in the lab and walked up through the garden. The snow was tinted yellow beneath the black sky. 'Spooky, innit?' Justin said. The echoing report of the TV became audible. The football results.

'Justin,' I said, 'I want you to do something for me.'

'What's that then?'

'I want you to become a skinhead.'

'Er?'

'I want you to have your hair cropped, okay? That's the only important part.'

'Fuck off. No one's a skin no more. My bruvver was a skin years ago but – '

'Just get your hair cropped. I don't mind what you call it.'

'I reckon you're losing your marbles, mate.'

'Please.'

'If you tell us why.'
'I'll explain later.'
'Shysters.'
Gail was in the kitchen. 'Spose you want some tea,' she said.
Justin glanced at her, patriarch and chauvinist already. 'Course we bloody do.'
'Language,' Gail said.
'Stupid cow,' he retorted as he stalked off into the back room.
Being well-bred I said, 'Thank you very much, Gail. I'd like tea very much.' ('In'ee nice your friend?' she was always saying to Justin.)
I followed through into the back room where Mr Burrows was checking off his pools coupon before the blaring TV. The room smelt of Woodbines, toasting crumpets and stale hair-oil.
'Mug's game,' Mr Burrows said. Scottish League Division Two was just starting but he already knew he hadn't won. He never put Scottish teams down for draws because the goalkeepers were too unpredictable or, as he termed it, 'a bunch of wankers'.
'How long have I been doing this? Eh?'
'Nineteen years, Dad.'
'And how much have I won?'
'Four-and-six, Dad.'
'And when was that?'
'1963, Dad.'
'Bollocks.' He threw the crumpled pools coupon across the room but it missed the wastepaper basket. 'Bollocks,' he repeated. He turned round and fixed his five-mild-and-bitters-at-lunchtime eye on me. 'Don't become a gambling man,' he solemnly instructed me.
'I won't, Mr Burrows.'
'Probabilities,' he said, derisively.

18

Norman Unbound

It was no sooner said than done. Justin's hair was shaved within a quarter inch of his skull. He looked more sinister than ever — more likely to come looming from a dark hole in a tunnel with Neanderthal-looking chums who beat down innocent passers-by for small change.

'Suits you very well,' I told him.

'Yeah, saul right.' He ran his fingers over the soft bristle. His face was more squat than before, crushed up as though he were a bulldog sculpted by successive generations of face-pounding. 'Dad's got a pair of red braces I'm gonna nick, and when I've got the bread I'm gonna get some Doc Martens.' He smacked his lips: *taystee*.

What was this potent power of persuasion I wielded over people of lesser intelligence? For years he had devoted his life to growing his hair as long and unruly as possible. He hid on Saturday mornings when his father threatened him with the barber. He wanted to emulate Chris who lived in Canada and christened his kids after Mick and Bianca Jagger. Being yourself.

A dozen words from me changed all that. He casually traded in identities. Already he was asking me to get some ink and tattoo the motto *Skins* on his arm. 'I don't think that'll be necessary, Justin. I don't think there's any need to spell it out for people. They'll get the message.'

'But it looks good, don't it?'

'Lovely.'

'Tasty.'

The reason I had asked Justin to become a skinhead was simple. It would come as no surprise to anyone when the easily influenced Norman followed suit. This he did just into the New Year. I returned from the barber with him (I had had my usual neatly parted JFK cut) and his ears glowed vivid pink in the cold. It had been a bit of a job persuading him, having to stand behind him and glare if he looked as though he was going to back out and ask the barber for his normal cut, but he seemed quite happy with the result. When we got to his home though Beth was not so happy.

Beth burst out crying. 'What have you done to yourself?' she warbled, and ran off to the kitchen to gobble some more Valium. Norman and I stepped into the house, wiped our feet, and were heading towards the cave when she appeared again and said, 'I don't know what your father's going to say. I just don't.' And disappeared once more.

I don't think this was something Norman had given much thought to in his moment of brash adolescent rebellion. His face went white, though his ears remained pink. Things were not as bad as once they had been with Keith. There were no longer Airfix models for Keith to smash up when he was angry, and his satisfaction in the use of the belt had diminished over the years. It had diminished on a sliding scale roughly antithetical to the sprouting of Norman's height, now a gangling five foot ten. The day Norman had overtaken the short, jauntystepped Keith had, in fact, been the day Keith stopped using the belt. None the less old associations die hard and Norman still could not suppress an unconscious quaking of the flesh when the wrath of Keith was invoked. Keith's hand so much as touching his belt still induced wobbling in Norman's chin.

We were in the cave, now a considerably more respectable dwelling, complete with the record player Norman had saved up his paper round money for. (I had stopped taxing him when Keith started asking embarrassing questions about where his money went.) Norman was sifting through his neatly stacked pile of LPs, these being by Black Sabbath, The Groundhogs, Deep Purple, The Cream, Uriah Heap and Norman's favourite band, Budgie. It was Budgie's 'Squawk!' that he selected after some deliberations. He dropped the needle down on to the record and there began a raucous stream of heavy-metal guitar solo.

This was Norman's usual occupation these days; this or going through one of his still-loved animal books, or both at the same time. He spent long hours in the cave with his library of heavy-metal blaring from the record player. Beth would be through in the living-room with a Mills & Boon, or simply gazing at the wall in a haze of Valium that made her quite content to do nothing for hours on end. She had never been a very active woman at the best of times, if ever there had been times in her life that could have been so described. Now she was passive in the extreme, finding it all she could do to stagger up in the morning and place the cornflakes on the table, and shove the Findus cod under the grill and the frozen peas in a saucepan in the evening. Very occasionally she would make it along the hall to ask Norman to turn the music down. He'd turn it down, then turn it back up again when she was back in the living-room. She'd take another couple of Valium and gaze at the carpet.

'So why did you want me to have my hair cut?'

'Sorry?' It was impossible to hear him above the noise.

'Er, like,' and he went and turned the volume down slightly. 'Why did you want my hair like this, like?'

'For the experiment. It will allow the current easier access to your brain.'

'Oh.' And he turned the music back up again. He didn't look exactly jubilant about the prospect.

'You don't mind, do you, Norm? About the experiments?'

'What?'

'You don't mind about the experiments? They're not causing you any discomfort?'

'Er, no. Fine, like,' and he mumbled a bit more, quite inaudible.

We sat like this for a while. It was somewhere in the middle of an ear-burning guitar solo that Norman saw through the window the approach of Keith's Capri. (He had moved up in the world, though it had cost him stomach ulcers.) Norman went over and took the arm off the record.

He always did this when Keith returned home in the

evening. We watched Keith in the light from the landing as he came bouncing up the path with his briefcase, swinging his key-ring round his fingers. Beth opened the door and said, 'You'd better go and see what he's done to himself.' The briefcase was dropped on the hall floor and Keith's footsteps could be heard coming down the passage. Even the sound of his feet angered me. I had long hated this man, sweaty business man, part-time sadist and smasher of Airfix models. I suppose the fact that he had fornicated with Alice added a certain edge to my loathing.

It was at this point that Norman surprised me. He leapt up from the bed, went to the door, opened it, stood for a second and said, with enormous calm, 'Hi, Dad. Have a good day at the office?'

Keith said nothing. He just stared in disbelief for a while. His aphony was broken only by my appearance in the door behind Norman at which point he said, 'Bloody hell,' and returned along the hall.

I seriously believe this was the first time in his life that Norman had managed to speak a whole sentence to his father without so much as the smallest stutter.

He turned back into the room now, and in a mood of defiance I had never imagined him capable of returned the arm on to the record. A pandemonious chorus of tortured-cat fuzzbox burst out into the house. He seized his old childhood cricket bat from the tea-chest and gripped it as if it were an electric guitar. He leapt up on to the bed and bounced up and down, thrashing wildly at the imaginary instrument. His face was contorted into a series of bizarre grimaces made all the more wonderful by his cropped scalp. Then he took the cricket bat into a new position and writhed up and down with it. I realised that it was supposed to denote a machine gun.

19

At the Bee Colony

'He was a wild beast, a crazed animal.'
'No shit?'
'A wild man, Justin. Merciless, brutal, savage.'
Justin was singing: '*Wild thing! (na na na na) You make my heart s* – ' Sing? Sink? Ping? He couldn't remember. 'Troggs, great band.' He jerked his neck for emphasis.
We were on a field trip of sorts with Miss Colley. She was in the final stages of preparing her doctorate thesis on the homing instincts of bees, and we had volunteered to come along and help out. Exactly how had not been specified. It was Justin's intention that we 'gang-bang' her. 'Na, you can see. She's really desperate for it. Most middle-aged birds are.'
'Justin, twenty-six is hardly middle-aged.'
'Course it is.'
We were tramping up a hillside, past a barn, along the side of a pungent-smelling bronze field. A Weetabix commercial. A fragrant warm wind blew up around us, lazy and aphrodisiac.
'She aint bad for an older bird. Better than that old dog I shacked up with behind the language block. Je-zus. Should've smelt her cunt.' At the top of the hill the wheat gave way to pasture. We were walking a short way behind Miss Colley. She strode confidently in her white mackintosh, a wicker basket of hermetically sealed jars swinging from her hand. 'Really moving her arse about,' Justin said. 'Anyway, what else did e do?'

It was nine months after Norman had defied Keith with the blast of music, about ten after the onset of the cybernetics research. Norman was a changing person.

'Growled. Growled like a Doberman. Smashed up one of the old engines in the garden. He was *mean*, Justin. You really should have been there.'

'Fuck.'

'He was straddling the carburettor, gritting his teeth, barking, pummelling it with a shovel. He bit through a light flex, the power wasn't on, fortunately. He tried karate chops on a pile of bricks. I knew I'd get this hypothalamus business sorted out in the end.'

'Shit.' Shaking his head in wonderment.

'He bent the handles on your dad's old wheelbarrow, tried to have a go at one of the snakes. I had to restrain him a bit there. I let him take it out on a bit of hosepipe. Then he decided he was going to go and fuck Gail.'

For a moment Justin seemed not to have heard. Then he had.

'*What!*'

'Oh, yes, as I say: a raging beast. He had quite a good go at it too, if I – '

'Fucking cunt, I'll kill im. Je-zus. What'd she do?'

'Wasn't too bothered really. I think she quite likes Norman. If it hadn't been for the fact that – '

'She was gonna let im?' Justin had stopped walking now and stood, simian arms dangling at his sides, grotesque incredulity carved into his face.

'Mm, looked like it. She was sort of tugging at her panties – she was on the kitchen table at this point, where Norman had cast her with his first onslaught – when, as I keep trying to tell you – '

'But Norman don't fuck birds, I mean . . . ' Words failed him.

'You boys all right?' Miss Colley had stopped and was calling in her hockey captain voice.

'Fine thanks, Miss Colley. Just coming. Justin's just a bit surprised at something I told him.'

'Oh, okee-doke,' and she turned and continued through the grass. From the ridge of the hill the beehives were just coming into sight, ordered rows of them far below like lines of sugar cubes on green baize.

'I mean, like, he just, when you'd, you know, taken the elmet off, he went down the ouse and tried to screw Gail?' Justin remained glued to the spot.

'Basically, yes. After he'd growled and bitten the light flex and all that, that is. That's pretty well it. They started by kissing in fact. Norman sort of threw himself at her, then started feeling her tits through her blouse, then – '

'You saw? Je-su!'

I began to walk on and he followed hypnotically: nothing would drag him from the oracle.

'What happened then?'

'A pan of sprouts fell off the table – Gail had just been making your dad's dinner and – '

'I don't wanna know about the fuckin dinner!'

'I was just giving some flesh to the narrative, Justin.'

'Did he get his cock out?'

'Um, yes. Partly. As I was saying he was prevented from finishing the job by – '

'I don't fuckin believe it.' His voice seemed to snap, to shift two octaves up on the second syllable of 'believe'. Miss Colley turned round again.

'Rarely Justin! Language!' He managed a small subliminal grunt of apology and clamped his hand to his forehead like a bemused cartoon character. 'And what is it you don't ef-ing believe, Justin?' He proved unable to frame a response.

'Well, Miss,' I said, 'Justin was just surprised by the results of an experiment I carried out. We were discussing my findings.'

'Oh, what was thert?' I wondered if it was the influence of the country air, of manure, clover and the ripe wheat that was producing this fiercely County accent.

'It was some work I've been trying to perfect for quite a long time now. Basically it involves using electricity – '

Justin seemed to wake up; at least, something inside him said that I should not be about to regale Miss Colley, a teacher *and* a bird, with an account of the artificial stimulation of the hypothalamus, and especially with its latest fruition, Norman's attempt to copulate with his sister. To stop me the first thing that came into his head was to fling himself on to the ground, grasp his thigh, and shriek the single word, 'Cramp!'

Miss Colley was rushing back down the field.

She believed that Justin was a martyr to cramp. Since his first use of the tactic the day we stole the snakes' eggs, he had many times reduced himself to a gibbering wreck in her company so she would have to massage his afflicted thighs. Many times had she urged him to see a doctor. At first he had declared that he distrusted all doctors since the one who operated on his mother to remove a gallstone and killed her. Eventually he agreed he would go and see a doctor, but he had not as yet done so. Each time he got the cramp he swore he would go the next day.

'Come along.' She was kneeling on the grass between his outstretched legs. 'Did you see a doctor as you said you were going to last time?' Stuck for an answer he resorted to another hideous moan. He gritted his teeth and squeezed his eyes up into tight little clusters. 'Better now?' she said, stood, and marched back towards her basket.

We walked slowly, allowing her to get ahead of us. After a while the sound of the bees became audible. When it seemed safe Justin spoke again, 'Gail was gonna let im?'

'Yes. Do I have to keep repeating myself?'

'So what happens? Why don't they?'

'Your dad came in.'

He stopped dead again. His eyes opened wide. 'Fuckin Ada,' he said. 'What's he do?'

'Just says could he have his dinner now please, if it's not too much trouble.'

'Gordon Bennett!' He shook his head.

Miss Colley had stopped again. 'Justin, you didn't tell me. Have you seen a doctor? About your cramp?'

We continued to walk towards her. He was silent. It seemed everything was conspiring against him. I looked at him and saw that his face had adopted a new posture. I stopped but he continued until he stood only a few feet from her. 'Yes, Miss,' he said, 'I've been to see the doctor quite a few times.'

'Yes? And?'

'I have something called arteriosclerosis, it's something to do with the blood. It's incurable.'

In all the possible roles I had ever cast him in that of doomed Romantic hero had never before been one of them.

An expression of overpowering sympathy came over Miss Colley's face. She dropped the basket of jars and took a step towards him.

'I don't expect to live long,' was the next thing I heard him say. She was running forward to take the doomed figure of Justin into her arms. (Perhaps all along there had been a reason for Justin's obsession with my book, *The Dictionary of Symptoms*. I had always thought it was just a ghoulish fascination, but it seemed that he had been learning. Recurrent cramp is a symptom of arteriosclerosis, though, of course, he suffered from neither.)

Her white mackintosh was crushed beneath her and Justin was on top, pawing rapaciously. Her hair had fallen out of its bun and splayed across her face like a statue of someone drowning. Justin showered kisses upon her and went to work upon the opening of her blouse. A spray of buttons flew into the grass. 'Could you be a bit more careful?'

'Sorry, Miss,' Justin said.

After hasty and awkward preparations Justin and I took it in turns making love to Miss Colley. I watched with a certain fascination the way his lean and taut buttocks went up and down, curt grunts issuing the while from his mouth. It reminded me very much of his hard-fought four hundred metres conquests on the school athletics track. He went at it with a megalomanial seriousness. I had forcibly to restrain my laughter. It transpired that he did indeed regard this as a competition to see who could pleasure the seemingly tireless Miss Colley the most times. It even occurred to me that he might have devised a scoring system akin to his complex tabulation of window-breaking.

Towards the end of the hour that the whole proceedings took he was to be seen, while I was atop Miss Colley, coaxing his penis into full tumidity. He was kneeling in the grass, looking down upon it as upon a disobedient animal. He was tapping it with the tips of his fingers and, if I was not terribly mistaken, *talking to it*.

Clothed again, we were walking to the bee farm. Justin was

talking about 'the replay'. Miss Colley, Sylvia as she had now instructed us to call her, had regained her wholesome hockey captain air.

As we began to walk down through the rows of hives Justin started to twitch. He kept swinging round and jumping up and down. Suddenly he started howling. 'Miss! Miss! The bees are aving a go at me!'

'Don't be so silly, Justin,' she chided him. 'If you jump about of course they will. Otherwise they're perfectly harmless.'

'They are, honest. They're trying to get up my leg.'

'You are a chump.'

'Really, I mean it. I reckon it's my sweat. They reckon it's pollen and nectar and that, like.'

We both laughed at this suggestion.

It was at this point that it began to dawn on me that she was not treating Justin with quite the air of solemn respect one would have for a nascent Keats or Chatterton. Justin seemed oblivious of this fact.

We arrived at the collection of wood and corrugated iron buildings that constituted the bee farm and Sylvia instructed us to remove our clothes. Justin looked frightened as she disappeared round the corner with the basket of jars. When she was out of earshot he said, 'What a bird, eh mate?'

I nodded.

She reappeared with a hosepipe which she attached to a lone cold tap at the side of one of the buildings. When we had undressed she turned the stream of freezing water upon us. After a few minutes of this Justin looked down at himself with an expression of horror. 'My balls have disappeared,' he said.

We were all togged up in the white apiarian suits. Safe now from the bees' prying investigations of his genitalia, Justin regained his old bravura. 'You can't get me now, you bastards,' he told them. Then he jumped around pretending he was an astronaut.

We were holding the jars into which Sylvia was scooping small spatulas of honey from each hive. When analysed these samples would reveal where the bees from each hive were gathering their food. This information would go into the construction of her vast map of the bee labyrinth, a concatenation of coloured lines like a diagram of aircraft corridors or the migratory patterns of birds.

'So when do you expect to die, Justin?' Sylvia said.

'Sorry? Oh, pretty soon. A year or two. I've got to go for these tests like, see, cos there's this new treatment they might be tryin on me. They have to take all my blood out, see, and put it all in this special machine that kind of, er, takes out all the furry bits that are kind of clog . . . '

He stopped now, aware that Sylvia was laughing.

'Oh,' he said. Something was slowly dawning on him.

'I don't think there'll be any reason for you to get cramp any more, will there?' Sylvia said.

'Er, no, Miss,' he replied.

20

Breakfast

It was breakfast the next morning, a Saturday. Alice was frying eggs in the Teflon non-stick pan. Upstairs Ken was solemnly donning his Marks & Spencer's gardening outfit in which to mow the lawn. I was laying the table for Alice.

Angus appeared, podgy-faced, from the hall. He was well-embarked now on his pimpled adolescence and had developed that desperate self-consciousness as regards matters of dress, hairstyle and elocution that seems to be the lot of people suffering from that condition. He had for the previous few weeks been working in the sly, insidious manner of the child to attain the things he felt would betoken his adulthood. These things were (1) a pair of loons and (2) a pair of platform shoes. He had been whining on to Alice about how he *needed* these objects. She had proved unable to comprehend this necessity. What was wrong with the trousers he already possessed? she demanded. But Angus had learnt fast how to utilise the classic defence strategy of the adolescent mind: Alice didn't *understand* him.

He found himself unable to articulate the humiliation he felt attending the Youth Centre fortnightly discos without the desired loons.

Alice had sought consultation with me on these matters. Why does Angus want horrid clothes like that? (Paul never did.) Why does he sulk so much? (Paul never did.) Why does he pretend he can't speak correctly? (Paul never did.) Why does he slouch? Why try and get his hair cut in such a ridiculous way? Does he really have to have that picture of Rod Stewart on the wall? (Paul did none of these things.)

'Well,' I explained, 'that's just part of growing up. Angus is going through his rebellious phase. He'll grow out of it, I'm sure.'

Alice had known to expect this rebellious phase from her offspring, she had just never imagined it could take such a grotesque form. She tried hard to suppress her desire to compare Angus aged thirteen with Paul aged thirteen. She remembered well Dr Spock's words on the subject of sibling comparisons. But try as she might the comparison soon found verbal expression the day, I think it was, that Angus first used the adjective 'groovy'.

'But, Mum,' I said, 'we're all different. Angus is just trying to express himself in his own way.'

This was a moot point, particularly with Ken.

Just what precisely was he trying to express? Ken said he had not felt this need for 'self-expression' when he was a youngster. Yes, he granted, he'd done his share of silly things. He and his friend, for instance, had drunk a bottle of cider up a tree in the vicarage garden. But he had never felt obliged to drawl and slouch and sulk the whole time.

'That's the trouble with so many young people nowadays,' he told me. 'That's the Welfare State. They think the world owes them a living.'

I agreed with him.

'You're not like that, of course. You know you've got to look out for yourself.'

'Thank you, Dad.'

'No! I mean it.' And he proceeded to praise me for my recent academic successes and the imminent possibility of my being awarded an early place at Oxford. 'Not that I'd want to compare Angus with you.'

'Of course not, Dad.'

We went on to discuss the current political climate. Ken expressed his heartfelt feeling that the abolition of national service was at the root of the problem. I agreed, electing not to point out that Angus was yet a mite too young for this useful discipline. He then went on to express his even more heartfelt conviction that Enoch Powell had the right ideas about things. Again I refrained from reminding Ken of the anguish he had felt when his political hero had urged the populace to vote Labour.

Ken was increasingly obsessed with the past. He spent long hours regaling me with tales of his youth and the wholesome values that had been associated with it. Our patio conversations were less and less concerned with science, more and more with Ken's golden age. It brought on a strange intimacy between us, and from this grew his increasing desire to tell me about his problems, specifically, his discovery now he was past forty that the world was failing to reward him as bountifully as he had once imagined it would. He bemoaned the fact that he had risen no higher in the company than he had. He reminded me a hundred times of the many valuable contracts he had acquired. It was palpably unfair that others had risen higher than he. (How long had I sat and bided my time, knowing that one day he would let slip *that* word?)

'But Dad,' I replied, quashing the smallest hint of irony from my voice, 'the world is an unfair place.'

He did not seem happy to be confronted with his own words of yesteryear.

Angus shuffled to the breakfast table wearing his habitual sneer. I came through from the kitchen and handed him his plate of eggs and bacon. Ken came and sat at the table.

'All right if I go down the football?' Angus said. You could almost hear Alice's teeth grinding together in the kitchen. She always ground her teeth at Angus's affectation of lazy speech. 'Dad?'

Ken said nothing as he chopped a careful square from his egg. He ate with great precision, wasting nothing. He looked with disgust upon Angus's plate, where the whites of the eggs were being sawn away because Angus didn't like the whites. When he was a lad he ate what he was given or went without. Alice was coming from the kitchen, Rachel following with the toast-rack held in her dainty little fingers. Alice looked imperious. This facial expression was the invariable prelude to a homily on Angus's poor powers of articulation.

'One goes *to* a football match, Angus, not down it.'

'Tch. You know what I mean though. What's it matter?'

'*Why* does it matter. And there is a *t* sound in matter.'

Ken now chose his moment to speak. 'Haven't you got anything better to get on with?'

Alice was daintily cutting the rind off her bacon and looking to see that Rachel wasn't playing with her food. She wasn't. 'Angus,' she said, removing the rind to the side of the plate, 'don't you think it's dangerous with all those football hooligans? You haven't done your arithmetic homework, have you?'

'I can do it tomorrer.'

'Your mathematics report was rather a disappointment last term, wasn't it? What was it again?'

'How should I know? I don't care.'

'I hardly think that sort of attitude is going to get you anywhere. But then, perhaps you don't mind. What did that report say again?' She seemed to search her mind for it.

'Very poor work throughout the year. He is lazy and temperamental in class. If he does not curb his slovenly behaviour he may find himself having to answer to the headmaster.' I knew it word for word.

'Yes, that was it. Thank you, Paul.'

'Angus, could you pass the marmalade please?' I smiled at him.

'You could do some of your painting rather than go to a football match,' Alice helpfully suggested.

'Yes,' I agreed, 'you could carry on with that Van Gogh picture you were doing. "Sunflowers", wasn't it?'

'What's it got to do with — '

'Don't be so rude, Angus!' Alice said. 'Paul was only making a civil suggestion. It's no wonder your teachers say — '

'He said he didn't like it!' Angus blurted.

'It's not finished yet. Far be it from me to comment on an unfinished work.'

'You should persevere,' Alice said.

Ken nodded. That was the problem — Angus never stuck at anything. 'Persevere' was one of Ken's buzz-words, guaranteed to illicit a favourable response, whatever the context.

'Don't feel like it.'

Alice made her tutting noise, looked at Angus while she disengaged a fibre of bacon from her teeth with her tongue, then said with surprisingly savage sarcasm, *'Feel like it?* Don't feel like it. Well what do you *feel* like doing, your lordship?' It was a tendency I had noticed increasingly throughout the preceding year, this way of snapping back at Angus with an acidic echo of his own words. It revealed a depth of vindictiveness I had not previously thought her capable of. I liked it.

Ken joined in. 'You won't get anywhere with that attitude, young man.'

'And you can stop sulking,' Alice added.

There was a momentary hiatus.

'Angus's picture's horrid,' Rachel piped up, marmalade on her chin.

'Rachel!' Alice said, 'don't be so nasty. You can go upstairs if you're going to say things like that.' Rachel had not yet grasped the full etiquette of Angus persecution.

'Just saying what I think,' she said, with sardonic innocence. 'Paul can paint much better than Angus can.'

'That'll do, I said. Paul is older than Angus is. Eat your toast.'

'Sorry.'

Rachel had a rare quality at this age. She was capable of making brilliantly incisive remarks of this nature and then demurely dismissing her own opinions with a graceful lightness of touch. Angus hated it. He detested the fact that his sister, a mere eight years of age, could so harass his fragile adolescent ego.

'Yes, Rachel,' I said, 'you mustn't discourage Angus. I think his "Sunflowers" is going to be a great success when it's finished.'

When breakfast was over Ken went out into the garden to assemble the Qualcast. I went upstairs to brush my hair and Angus followed Alice through into the kitchen to whine for money for the football. 'You'll have to ask your father. I don't think it's a good idea though.' He came out of the kitchen and slunk upstairs to play his Mud record and pick at his pimples.

This was a very average sort of Saturday breakfast.

21

Observations

After a short chat with Ken about a lawn-mower malfunction I went straight round to the lab. Justin was already there, and we moved the snakes out into the greenhouse extension so as to take the opportunity of cleaning out their aquarium.

Justin could talk of nothing but the events of the previous day and Norman's attempted coupling with Gail. Sometimes as he spoke the two subjects ran straight into one another. 'What an incredible chick,' would merge immediately with another expression of his incredulity regarding Norman and Gail. It transpired that he had broached the subject with her immediately upon returning home the previous evening. To his utter dismay Gail had said she thought Norman was 'quite cute'. He still couldn't get it out of his head that Norman wasn't supposed to be interested in that sort of thing.

In consequence of this he announced that he would have to make some modifications to the car seat. 'I can't risk im doin that again. She's my fucking sister,' he said. The disparity between this sentiment and his praise for Sylvia never once seemed to occur to him.

He was welding a new attachment on to the car seat, brilliant showers of blue and white spraying up round his arms. He said something but I was unable to hear it through the visor. He lifted the visor and spoke again. 'What I can't suss out is how she knew about the cramp and that all the time. I mean, she never said nuffin all those times I got er to rub my legs. I mean, you'da thought she'd ave been really fucked off about that.' He pulled the visor down again and went to work on the other arm of the chair.

It was beginning to look more and more like something from *A Shorter History of Torture*. The new attachment was a bar that could be swung into place around Norman's waist, so restraining him from escaping in the event of his managing to break through the three-inch steel band. It was also Justin's intention to attach a manacle to the wall and secure this round Norman's ankle during the experiments. The welding stopped again and he removed the visor.

'I tell ya what,' he said, 'd'you reckon she knew even that time when we nicked the snakes' eggs?'

I have to admit this was a possibility that had not previously occurred to me.

'Na,' he said, 'she'd've done something about that.' But he sounded far from sure.

I went to clean out the aquarium. Justin began welding again. He had not been doing this long when he leapt into the air and lurched across the floor with the oxy-acetylene still burning in his hand. He was struggling to extinguish the flame and at the same time trying to yell something at me through the visor. His free arm swung wildly in many directions; towards the bench, towards the anatomical diagram pinned to the wall, towards a rack of frog urine samples. I reflected that his behaviour had been increasingly erratic over the last few months and that I must have a word with him about this. Finally, he got the visor off and the last syllable of his intended utterance escaped: 'Ey!'

In the event it proved sufficient.

I ran to the door and shouldered it open, stumbled and nearly fell through the glass of the greenhouse extension. As I was regaining my balance I saw her, no more than ten yards away. I continued to run until our bodies met in a fierce inosculation that threw her down into a bed of run-to-seed rhubarb plants. I fell on top of her, my arms entangled with her handbag and the belt of the white mackintosh. In a gesture of self-protection her fingers had gone up and torn at my face. 'Miss Colley,' I said, unable to think of anything more appropriate to the circumstances. Then, still unable to think of anything that would begin to justify my conduct, I began to kiss her.

'Really, Paul,' she kept trying to say, but I would block her mouth again. My mind was filled with horror at the prospect of her going into the lab and seeing its arsenal of brutal-looking equipment. It was filled with even more horror at the prospect of her having already seen the snakes.

This had not lasted very long when I looked up and saw Mr Burrows standing over us. He was dressed in his garage mechanic's overalls, dribbles of black oil smeared down the legs, and carried in his hand a spanner some eighteen inches long. He held this like a Red Indian tomahawk. His forehead was creased with a series of bizarre, inquisitorial wrinkles, his jaw hardened into cuboid severity. His teeth were gritted and visible.

'I thought you were at work, sir,' I said, without moving.

He said nothing.

The three of us seemed to remain in these positions for some time. It was when Justin emerged ashen-faced from the lab that Mr Burrows began upon his lengthy tirade. He spoke in a voice that seemed expressionless and bland of necessity lest the smallest shock rupture the balloon of his vast wrath. He added emphasis where he felt it was necessary by giving a small gesture with the spanner.

He listed first the things Justin and I had stolen from his house: tea-caddy, motorcycling jacket, electric fires (2), cigarettes ('I count them, you know,' he said with proud northern meanness), methylated spirits, weedkiller, toilet water sprays ('of some sentimental value, though I don't suppose I should expect you to understand that' – they had been his wife's), radio components, George VI embroidered tea-cosy, lengths of hosepipe, razor-sharpening strop, fusewire, Gail's hairpins (Justin interrupted: 'She said I could ave em', but was silenced with a thrust of the spanner), hammer, screwdrivers, Crown Derby teacups, baking tin, home-made wine apparatus, Mrs Burrows's old hair-drier, loft insulation, electric blanket, magazine rack, clock, potato-peeler, bucket and *Whitaker's Almanack*.

'In addition to which', he continued, 'I cannot recall on how many occasions you have disturbed me, rushing through the house at all hours and — and where's that friend of yours? The one I found on the kitchen table? I'd most certainly like to have a word with him as well.'

'Dad, I can explain — '
'Can you? I should like to hear it.'
'Don't get all sarky wiv me.'
'How dare you speak to m — '
'Look! I said I could — '
'You keep it shut!'
'Excuse me,' Sylvia said.
'Yes?'
'I wonder if I might — '
'Am I to understand that you are these boys' teacher? Eh?'
'That is c — '
'It's a disgrace!' He now turned his glare upon me. 'Can you tell me what your young friend was doing with my daughter in my kitchen? Can you?'
'It's bloody obvious, aint it, Dad?'
'I told you to keep quiet!'
'I'm allowed to talk, aren't I?'
'You'll speak when you're spoken to.'
'Fuck off.'
'What did you say? *What did you say?*'
'You eard.'
'If you ever speak to me in that way again I'm going to — '
'*Please!*' screamed Sylvia.
' — D'you hear?'
'Loud and clear, honoured Pater.'
'You're a degenerate little gutters — '
'PLEASE!'
' — pe.'

Sylvia was crying. She had pushed me off her and stood up. She was trembling inside the mackintosh. Mr Burrows remained standing but his face had become a livid mauve. Blotches of it seemed to protrude as if the membrane of some grotesque toad. He was shaking with anger. 'Am I to understand that you are the boys' teacher?' he asked again.

'If you'd had the manners to listen you would already have gathered that.' She was visibly upset.

'Well, I'm sorry, i – '

'I fail to see how you can expect your son to behave well when you are the most ill-mannered man I have ever met.'

Justin released a small whoop of joy at this point. Angered, Mr Burrows sprang to his own defence. 'Well, it's no place of yours to come snooping round my – '

'I live ere too!' Justin bellowed.

'Not any longer you don't. I want you out tomorrow.'

'Fine. I'll pack now.'

'Oh no you don't. We've the other business to sort out first. Your "laboratory".'

He savoured the last word. I froze solid with fear.

He was gesturing with the spanner again. 'You!' he addressed me, 'What do you suggest I do first? Ring your father or ring the schoolteachers who think you're such a clever little bugger? I'm sure they would be interested to see your "laboratory". Don't you think?'

I found myself unable to speak.

It was Justin who spoke. 'Come on then, Dad, let's go and telephone. We haven't got nothin to hide.'

'Oh, I think you have.'

'No, Dad. Come along.'

And we were walking back up towards the house. My mind had gone completely blank. I stared at the gutted car radios, tyres and half-incinerated corn beef cans that littered the overgrown garden. As we walked Sylvia's foot caught on an old fizzy drink bottle concealed in the grass. It turned upwards, revealing a promise of 3d. for its return, and issued a thick slime of decaying matter from its throat.

When we reached the house we stopped. Mr Burrows instructed us to remain as we were and gestured Justin into the house. They both disappeared through the kitchen door.

22

Further Observations

I can hear – voices in a nightmare – Ken and Alice. Ken is furious, Alice is a jibbering, sobbing wreck. Ken is bellowing, 'How long has this been going on? How long?'
    Choking, Alice is joining in. 'What made you do it? You were doing so well at school. I don't understand. I just don't understand.'
    'Don't upset yourself,' Ken says.
    'But ... but ... Oh, Paul! Paul ... ' And her voice continues in a succession of sobs and gurgles.
    The voice of Dr Joseph joins the mélange. He is not angry the way Ken and Alice are. He is just heartbroken.
    'You were the most talented pupil I ever taught,' he says. 'We had such hope for you. Such promise. Why ... ? Why?'
    And I cannot answer.

After a short while Justin and his father appeared in the back room and stood a couple of yards from the telephone. They appeared like dumbshow silhouettes. I became aware that they were arguing about something.
    Sylvia cleared her throat. 'Well,' she said, 'I still haven't told you why I came round.' Given the circumstances there was a jangle of desperately false jollity in the way she spoke.
    'No.'
    'It's rather bad news, I'm afraid.'
    'I had the feeling it would be.'

'Look, is there anything I can do to help? What have you been doing down there?'

I could see no further point in lying. 'Justin and I stole a few things from school. Some chemicals and test-tubes and things. I think we're going to be in rather a lot of trouble.' Despite everything I omitted to mention the snakes and the artificial stimulation of the hypothalamus. I don't think I could have borne her knowing about all that.

'Oh dear. We wondered who'd been doing that.'

'Now you know.'

'I'm sure it's not as serious as you think. I don't expect . . . ' and she seemed to be at a loss for words.

'Anyway, tell me why you came here.'

'Yes, well, I've er lost my job. Because of what happened yesterday. He saw us. Up at the farm.'

For a moment I didn't understand what she was saying.

'Sorry?'

'He saw – '

'The Head of Science?'

'Yes.'

'He saw us at the bee, er . . . ?'

'Yes.'

I remembered the many hours we had spent together. Images of the Head of Science and me, of feeding tanks full of brilliantly coloured tropical fish, pinning butterflies on the baize trays, dissecting rats, welled up in my thoughts.

'It's not the end of the world, you know,' Sylvia said. 'I don't imagine things will be helped when he knows about Justin and you stealing those things though.'

'He sacked you? Just like that?'

'He said it risked the school's good name.'

'I don't think he had any right to do that.'

'Well, he's going to give me a reference for another job.'

'But what right is it of his? What's it to do with him?' I was furious.

'You have to see it from his p – '

But she never finished speaking. Justin came dashing through the door. 'Quick! Scarper, Miss!' he yelled and pointed her towards the path that ran down the side of the house. 'Please. Go away. It's really urgent.'

'But Justin – '

'Don't argue! Just go!'

And she found herself being physically removed towards the gate. 'We'll talk later. Honest. You've just gotta go. Goodbye!' he called, and she had disappeared around the house. Justin rushed back in a frenzy of activity.

'Right, mate. Don't say nuffin.'

I tried to speak.

'No! Just move. We've gotta clear that shed out now. And I mean now, man!' He was running down the garden towards the shed. I chased after him and he disappeared into it. Before I could follow him in he had re-emerged with a shovel. 'Start digging!' he yelled, throwing the shovel at me.

'Where?'

'Anywhere, you cunt. Just do it!'

And before I could speak again he was back in the shed tearing things off the walls, heaving things out of the door in a rapid flurry of activity.

I started digging.

An hour later we had buried everything we had ever stolen and dismantled the entire laboratory. All I had got out of Justin was that he didn't think his father was now going to inform the school authorities about the stolen goods. Nor did he think – 'I can't promise this, mate' – that he was going to contact Ken and Alice. He refused to tell me how he had managed to engineer this. 'Maybe I'll tell ya later, mate. Just keep fuckin diggin, will ya?'

I had of course to tell Justin that I had told Sylvia about some of our thefts. He stopped still, standing over the hole with a flagon of nitric acid in his hands. 'You are a bleedin headcase, mate, that's what you are. Why the fuck did you tell er? Je-su!'

'I thought, I thought they'd know soon enough – '

'You didn't trust me. You need your ead examining.'

I went on to tell him about her losing her job because the Head of Science had driven up to the bee farm and seen us. A vast smile broke out across his face. 'There is hope yet, my son,' he said.

When we had finished filling in the hole and attempting to disguise it with dead bracken and sheets of old corrugated iron, he announced that he would go straight round and find Sylvia. 'She really likes me, mate. I reckon I can persuade her not to say nuffin. Specially as she's lost er job and that. I mean, she's on our side now, don't ya reckon?'

I reckoned she was.

While he did this I was to dispose of the snakes. Neither of us had been prepared to bury them with all the other spoils of our thieving. 'Yeah,' he said, 'you find a nice home for em, mate. I'll miss them snakes. Good blokes they are. Shame we never got em to have any babies.'

'They're both boys, Justin.'

'Yeah, I know that. What d'you think I am? Thick or something? Yeah, I tell ya what. There's that nice little copse next to the Porters's garden. I reckon they'd like it there.'

'That's where I'll take them,' I said, quite automatically.

'Right, let's fuck off. I'll see ya later. Don't worry, we'll be all right.'

He started walking up the garden and I followed him, the snakes in a suitcase in my hand.

'Good luck!' I called after him as he disappeared down the road on his old bicycle.

23

The Head of Science

I did not go to the copse near the Porters's garden. I went straight to the bus-stop and caught a bus to the school. It was my practice to go into the school on Saturday mornings to work and to grovel to the Head of Science. He always went in on Saturday mornings to play with his collection of butterflies and feed the laboratory mice. Sometimes he practised his putting on the carpet of the office, free from his wife's nagging.

He told her that he spent this time working on the updated version of his *Survey of Botany*. He had been claiming this for at least as long as I had known him, but the work progressed barely at all. He was happier just relaxing and playing with whatever animals he might happen to have at the time: the snakes which he had once possessed but had since given to the reptile house at Whipsnade; the lizards he kept at another time; or the monkeys he had been keeping for the last few months.

The monkeys were minute creatures no more than eighteen inches tall. The Head of Science had had the idea that he could train them to perform a variety of jobs such as putting on the kettle and making a cup of coffee, opening doors and fetching golf balls that strayed under the office furniture. He had seen this as the means by which he would make his fortune and so be able to give up teaching. He would simply market them to cripples and the bedridden.

The monkeys turned out to be less enthusiastic about this scheme of things. They rebelled violently against his instructions and frequently turned upon him with their razor-sharp teeth and their tiny needle-like claws. One monkey, endowed with a particularly great sense of initiative, threw a bottle of acid at him. To suppress this rebelliousness he tried many techniques. He locked the rebel in its cage and left it there without food for a week. Only when the beast was too weak to stand did he feed it. It fed and when it was strong enough rebelled again, surprising him by turning suddenly during the performance of some duty and digging claws and teeth into his thigh.

In the end there was only one solution to the problem. He designed a harness which was padlocked round the monkey's waist and groin. No amount of determination and ingenuity on the part of the monkey could remove the harness, which carried inside it a battery and a small prong that delivered an electric shock, operated by remote control from a device the Head of Science kept at all times in his jacket pocket. When a monkey got violent or persistently disobeyed an instruction he knew it understood, he flicked the switch. The effect was quite dramatic. The creature writhed about on the floor with its hair standing on end. Because of his short-sightedness he sometimes pressed the wrong switch and Monkey B was punished for the sins of Monkey D. In consequence of this they learnt a certain rather brutal camaraderie.

They also learnt to obey orders and the work progressed rapidly. The Head of Science had a training schedule worked out and every evening he set about teaching the monkeys a new task. 'Ah! Paul,' he would hail me, 'come and look at Clarence,' (Monkey C). 'He has learnt how to operate the tape recorder. This really is most encouraging.'

In the office Clarence sat on a bench with the tape recorder by his side. His big brown eyes looked terrified the way the monkeys' eyes always did. 'Now, watch,' the Head of Science said. 'I wish to dictate!' he declaimed.

Clarence looked at him, hesitated, and pressed a button on the machine. It went into Fast Forward.

'Dictate!' the Head of Science reiterated. 'Damn this animal, it had it a minute ago. *Dictate*, Monkey C!'

Clarence pressed Rewind and the tape ground to a halt, spluttered a little and started back.

'Stop!' And this time he got it right. 'Now, again. I – wish – to – dic – tate.'

This time Clarence remembered to press Record but also pressed Fast Forward. The tape recorder started squeaking.

'He is deliberately disobeying, he had it correctly a moment ago,' the Head of Science assured me and pressed Switch C on his gadget. Clarence went into palpitations and fell prostrate across the tape recorder. Sparks leapt out from the machine. Then it blew up, blowing Clarence up with it. The other monkeys looked impassively on as bits of tape and bits of Clarence were strewn about the office.

Undeterred, the Head of Science had the other monkeys get out the dustpan and brush to sweep up the mess. But it was in effect the end of the project.

When I got off the bus the Head of Science's was the only car parked on the grey asphalt. I walked past it with the suitcase swinging from my hand.

I walked up the stairs reading the graffiti carved into the grey paintwork: *Miss Colley is a Slut*; hypothetical football scores – *Chelsea 1000 West Brom 0*; rock song lyrics; and *Pete woz ere 16/2/75*.

As I walked down the corridor I noticed all the familiar smells. The disinfectant, stale polish, mice, algae, sulphur and, as I approached the door of his laboratory, the Head of Science's St Bruno. I went through the lab and noticed on the windowsill the preserved internal organs of a recently dissected frog.

I tapped three times on the door. There was a short pause, then his voice, 'Cmin.'

I entered. 'Good morning, sir.'

He was in the far corner by a cage of mice. He enjoyed feeding them individual seeds to see the way they would fight over them. He liked the high-pitched little noise they made when he stood over the cage and dangled the food before them. 'Sit down, Paul. With you in a moment.'

I put the case down and remained standing. With his back still turned he spoke again. 'Am I to understand that you have seen Miss Colley and that you have come wishing to explain your behaviour yesterday afternoon?'

'Yes, sir.'

'I see.' He remained with the mice a while longer, then swivelled round and walked towards his desk. 'Do sit down,' he repeated.

He began to fumble in his pocket for the pipe, then realised that he had left it by the mouse cage. He returned to fetch it, took it to the waste bin and tapped it against the metal. There was a small ravine of black ash down the side. He went back to his desk, took out his knife and started scraping it round the bowl of the pipe. 'I said you could sit down,' he said. 'And what is that suitcase you have there?'

'I was just using it to carry the results of some experiments, sir.'

'Going to rain, is it?'

'I don't know, sir.'

'Mm.' He sat on his swivel chair now and started packing his pipe. This he took some time over before lighting the pipe on one of his England's Glory matches. Then he said, 'Oh dear. This is most sad.'

'Sir.'

'I am afraid that the Headmaster has had to be informed because of the, the er – '

'The dismissal of Miss Colley, sir?'

'Precisely. That was of course er, that decision had to be taken by the Head.'

'Sir.'

He sucked now on the pipe. I could hear the crackle of the saliva.

'The Head has however expressed his wish that I should deal with this matter as it relates to yourself and your friend as, as it were, your Head of Department.' He scratched the side of his nose. 'This is a delicate matter. In the normal course of events it would not be any concern of the school's what you choose to do in your own time but, as I am sure you are aware – are you sure you wouldn't rather sit?'

'I would prefer to stand, sir.'

'Yes. I'm sure I don't need to inform you, Paul, that you have risked damaging the good name of the school by what you have done in a place where – where the public's gaze may have been upon you.'

The pipe had gone out. He fumbled with the matchbox.

'We all', he continued, 'have sexual er urges, and sometimes these urges may lead us to behave with an impropriety we would usually not er ... There is a time and place for everything and it is the function of our better selves to know — to judge what is right and proper ...'

'Sir.'

'Miss Colley has requested that I be lenient with you and your er friend. She has assured me that there was no — no undue er — that she was a willing partner in your activities.'

'That was very kind of her, sir.'

'Indeed. I have taken her word for this and presumed that you and your friend were — were momentarily swayed against your better judgments. Then again, it takes two to, to tango.'

'Three, sir.'

He was puffing on the pipe. 'Well, yes,' he said, ignoring the suggestion of facetiousness in my voice. 'Yes, indeed.'

(For most people life is a series of Hobson's choices. Their lives are moulded by the flux of circumstances.

What I was experiencing at this moment was to be no more than a mild ruction in the smooth path of determined events. Justin, it seemed, had succeeded in silencing his father on the subject of the lab. The Head of Science was taking a lenient view of my misdemeanour. The worst I would suffer on this score would be disapproving looks from Alice and another one of those man-to-man chats with Ken. Beyond that everything would progress as planned.

As a child prodigy I had excelled in large quantities of examinations. I was now awaiting news of my application to Oxford but my success in this was as predictable as all my other successes had been. There was nothing likely to incommode my stealthy ascent of the academic ladder. There had been nothing ever since the day I discovered the meaning of the word 'intelligence'; the day when, aged three, I was walking to Christine's party with Alice and I recombined the various parts of her many utterances on the subject of Justin and his family.

So everything was virtually arranged. Life stretched out before me, a series of easily predictable events, of choices strictly demarcated by the circumstances my intellect had prescribed. Probably since the first day that Dr Joseph perceived my precocious talent and went about arranging special tuition and promotion to a higher form all of this had been almost inevitable. And I had played no active part in deciding that this should be. I had merely done what was required. I had worked hard. Grovelled hard. Responded to the vanities and avarices of others. It had cost me very little effort and had suited perfectly my purposes. I would progress to university, become a research student of some description and then assume some lucrative academic post or work in a research institute.

It was not that I could not do otherwise, but that I would not. I had never shown the least inclination to dispute the dictates of circumstance. Decision-making in the future, as in the past, would be confined to the smallest of details. It would never take me outside the parameters dictated by my abilities and the process I found myself being subjected to.)

I stepped back and picked up the suitcase, undid the lock and held the case at arm's length. I secured my fingers round the lid so as to be able to lift it up. I threw the case across the room and the lid sprang open. I ran directly from the office, slamming the door shut behind me.

24

Hospital

The next thing I remember is sitting down in the car-park. Everything went grey, then black, and a loud buzzing filled my head. I was aware of the asphalt feeling damp against my face, then of one final sound: the merry jingle of an ice-cream van.

My name was being called. It was Alice and I was a little boy again, playing in the garden. She'd been out. It was a dry day and she'd left the washing on the line, and I had filled up the watering can and gone along with it and the step-ladder, watering the washing. She'd come home early and caught me and I couldn't excuse my action. 'Angus went for a wee-wee on it,' I said, 'I was trying to wash it again.' Then I remembered Angus hadn't been born yet. I ran away up the garden, trampling over the herb garden. The rich smell of the parsley and marjoram came up and filled my nostrils. 'Paul . . . ! Paul . . . ! Paul . . . !' Alice was shouting. I turned and could not see her through the parachute shapes the wind billowed the sheets into.

Then I was awake again. Right next to my eyes was the deep patina of a brown leather shoe. I looked up and saw Dr Joseph's yellow Brillo pad bobbling up and down. 'Paul, are you all right? What happened?'

'Felt faint,' I said, 'had to lie down.'

'Can you get up?'

'I . . . I . . . I . . .'

In the next dream I was surfing. I seemed to have to make no effort. Walls of water cascaded up around me. There was music, as though I was in a film. Seagulls flew overhead, chirping wildly. I was going somewhere beautiful.

When I woke up I had forgotten everything that had happened. I lay with my eyes closed for a while, as was my habit when I knew the first thing that would confront me was Angus's sleeping visage, the little encrustations of sleep that formed around his eyes, the way his ill-formed little mouth gaped when he slept. Then I remembered.

The adrenalin rushed right through to the roots of my hair. I thought perhaps the whole thing had been a very bad dream, that today had never happened, that I had dreamt tomorrow. But everything conspired to dissuade me from this idea: the whole sequence of events from Sylvia's arrival at the lab through to that moment when I stood on the Head of Science's carpet and let loose the suitcase and the snakes.

Immediately I started trying to think up excuses. I would claim I had found the snakes living in the wild and that I had recognised them as the highly dangerous king brown. I had laid a trap for them and taken them to the Head of Science, knowing him to be an expert. The suitcase dropped out of my hand and in my terror I fled the room. Some time passed as I devised these schemes, all of them seeming more and more inadequate as I conceived them. I contemplated with horror the prospect of the Head of Science having been bitten. That he might be dead was a possibility so awesome I could not entertain it without a wave of nausea sweeping over me.

I knew I was in hospital. From the smells and the feel of the coarse linen against my skin I had deduced that much. But how long I had been like this and who might be in the room with me, these things I could not discover. Hearing no sound in the room, I decided to risk opening my eyes.

I was in a tall, empty room with a dim yellow light on the far wall. Visible through the partially open door were the stockinged legs of a seated woman. A nurse. The sky outside the window was pale grey. It must be dawn. A whole night had passed. Everything would be known. It struck me now that it was possible no one did know. It was Dr Joseph who had found me in the car-park. The Head of Science might be lying dead in his office unbeknown to anyone. This struck me as a perfectly feasible possibility, and yet I could not seriously imagine it. The idea that I could actually have killed him was somehow remote, the sort of thing it just did not seem possible could have happened to me.

When I heard footsteps coming down the corridor I closed my eyes and listened. It was Ken's voice that I heard.

'Has he woken up yet?' he whispered.

It struck me as amazing that he should care.

'He's still asleep,' the nurse said. Her voice was pretty. 'I'll call you as soon as he wakes up.'

Ken whispered something else and then returned down the corridor. You could feel how he was being careful with his big, clumping feet. It seemed only reasonable that they had not yet found the body. How else explain the lack of anger in his voice? The prospect of the coming morning now filled me with a new horror. They would all come piling in with flowers, chocolates, grapes and paperbacks for the invalid, and I would have to sit up in the bed and tell them. The words seemed to form in my mouth: 'You are wasting your sympathy on a murderer.' I could see those blue veins on Alice's temples standing out to their full extent. Her whole world was shattered. Ken's whole world was shattered. Everything they had lived for seemed now to dissolve before this one terrible fact. How would they live with it? How could any of the ritual of their old life hold up in the face of the one bald and dreadful fact of my having murdered the Head of Science?

I opened my eyes again and screamed. The nurse came rushing through into the room. I kept screaming, staring into her face and baying like a deranged animal. As she was jabbing the needle into my compliant arm it occurred to me that I recognised her. As the buzzing filled my ears again and I dimly made out the figures of Ken and another nurse filling the doorway, I realised that she was Christine. The buzzing grew louder and I lost consciousness.

It was a long time before I awoke again from a deep and dreamless sleep. As I opened my eyes I looked up into the faces of Christine and Dr Joseph. They seemed to gaze at me with unfathomable depths of sympathy. How much more easily I could have borne their anger and hatred.

They were talking to me, or about me, I couldn't tell which.

They spoke as though I were not present there with them. 'It's been a tiring period for him,' Dr Joseph was saying.

'It must have been. Poor thing.' Christine now ran her cold hand over my forehead and brushed the damp hair away from my face. I stared at her. She was a real nurse with a watch pinned to her bosom with a big nappy pin. 'I'm going to go and get your parents,' she said.

She was gone. 'How are you feeling now?' Dr Joseph asked nervously. I was staring at his unshaven face, unable to speak. I tried and a grunting noise issued forth. 'Don't tire yourself,' he was telling me. I kept croaking at him and he was trying to push me back on to the pillows. 'All right, all right,' he said.

'Please!' I got out. 'I didn't mean it to happen.'

'Sssssh. Don't exert yourself.'

'You must listen!' I told him. I sounded delirious. My mouth felt as though it was filled with dough.

'There, there. There's no need to talk.' Christine had returned. Ken and Alice (*parents of the killer and former prize-winner*) stood behind her.

'No. Must talk.'

'He's still a little delirious,' Christine was telling Alice. Alice's eyebrows were all screwed up to express how distraught she was.

'Not, mind perfectly rational.'

Again her fingers ran over my forehead.

'Ger – '

'Sssssh.'

'Gre . . . ag . . . '

Ken and Alice were beaming down at me with the full thrust of their parental love.

'Ga . . . '

The next thing I was aware of was Alice talking in hushed tones to another nurse. Christine and Dr Joseph had gone. I sprang up from the bed and spewed forth a stream of incomprehensible noise. Both figures turned and smiled torrentially. The nurse was easing me back on to the pillow.

'Nightmares,' she said, turning to Alice. There was still no opprobrium in their voices.

'I'm perfectly well now,' I said.

'You will be. Would you like some tea now?'
I suddenly saw it all. This was the beginning of therapeutic treatment designed to destroy my murderous instincts.
'What have you put in it?' I screamed.
'Tt tt, silly. It's just ordinary tea.' The nurse appeared amused. Alice appeared terrified.
'Sorry, didn't mean it,' I grunted. 'What day is it?'
'It's Sunday. Now, you sit back and relax. Come along.'
She went for the tea and Alice sat holding my hand. She did not seem to know whether she should speak to me. 'I'm sorry for everything,' I told her. She smiled without signs of having comprehended me. When the nurse had returned and given me my tea they retreated out into the corridor for a whispered conference. I tried to hear what they were saying but couldn't. Then they came back in.
'I've got some very good news for you,' Alice said.
He wasn't dead?
Ken was in the room too. 'Have you told him yet?' he asked.
'We were just going to.'
Ken grinned ecstatically, and crossed his arms.
'Do you want to hear it now, sweetheart?' Alice asked.
'Yes, Mum. I feel fine.' I smiled with all my might.
And it was then that Alice told me about my scholarship to Oxford. 'Isn't that good news?' she said. I tried hard to summon up some joy suitable to the occasion but could not manage it.
'The school got the letter on Friday and Dr Joseph very kindly said he'd drive out to that place where you were, but . . . well . . . '
For a few moments what Alice was saying made no sense to me. She had gone slightly pink. Then I understood. It was Dr Joseph who had been out to the bee farm. It was he who had seen us. Ken and Alice, as witnessed by the embarrassment the subject was so obviously causing Alice, knew what had happened there.
I stayed awake now. After some more enthusing over my scholarship Ken and Alice went off to get something to eat. I requested something to read and the nurse, not wishing to overtax me, brought a selection of magazines from one of the waiting-rooms. She made me eat some pills. I stared at the

pictures in *Country Life*. The paper smelt odd; glossy and faintly bitter. In a women's magazine I read a few simple paragraphs about the domestic arrangements of astronauts in space: what and how they eat, how they exercise and perform Nature's calls. I examined an offer for four L.S. Lowry prints. I read *Which?* magazine on washing machines and the dangers of Hong Kong-manufactured cuddly toys. There were pictures of the various pieces of metal, the springs and pins that had come out of them. A 3-year-old child had recently been blinded by a koala bear. I scrutinised an advertisement for a mail order lingerie catalogue.

I then read with some impatience an article entitled 'Conditions in Today's Prisons' and contemplated the possibility of my own detention in one of them. I had become quite engrossed in this when I looked up and saw the Head of Science standing at my bedside.

'You're not dead?' I said.

He roared with laughter.

I was struggling to stand up but the buzzing started again. He was trying to help me back into the bed. The nurse was telling me how bad I was.

25

Justin Sells the Mice

After a few days I was allowed home. I spent the days sitting in bed. Morning and evening Alice brought the bottle of antibiotics and watched with gleeful solicitude as I ate them. She forbade me reading material any heavier than Ken's *Daily Express*, so the days were passed in apathetic games of Scrabble and Monopoly with Angus or Rachel. As each day passed I wondered more and more what had happened. Why had the Head of Science said nothing about the snakes? How had Justin managed to silence his father on the subject of the laboratory?

Sometimes I feared that Ken and Alice knew all about this but were saying nothing until I was well again. I searched their faces for signs of their knowledge but saw nothing. It occurred to me that the Head of Science might be waiting to tell them; similarly Mr Burrows. I could not believe the apparent peace that had settled on my life. Every morning when Alice came in with my tea I looked up into her face but nothing ever changed. In the evenings Ken came in and told me about his day. 'You'll be up and about in no time,' he told me.

Both of them had nothing but undying affection for me. Hardly a minute passed in which they did not congratulate me on gaining my scholarship. 'It's what you've always wanted, isn't it?' Alice said.

One evening Ken appeared home with a bottle of Champagne. He made a great ceremony out of opening it in the garden, then Alice and he came through to my room and we all had a glass. Alice would giggle when the bubbles went up her nose. Angus said he didn't like it. Ken had got it cheap from a customer.

The next day I was playing Scrabble with Angus. I felt so bad about always winning that I was actively trying to lose. I knew how much it would flatter his vanity if he once beat me. But when I looked at the expression of smug bliss on his face as he totted up the scores I found myself unable to suppress my desire to beat him. I always think I could better have borne his pleasure if it had not manifested itself in such an unpleasant facial expression. It was not as if he just actively gloated; he tried to repress the outward display of that gloating and it gave rise to that pinched, mean little look that Alice also had when she was happy about something.

I took my go. 'Quetzals,' I said.

'Don't believe you,' he stated.

'Look it up then.'

He looked it up.

'Correct me if I'm not mistaken, Angus. A central American bird and the monetary unit of Guatemala?'

'How come you always get the high-scoring letters?'

'I don't. It's just that when you do you can't think of any words.'

'It's not fair,' he moaned.

'Nuffin's fair, my son,' came the reply. I nearly jumped out of my skin. 'It's an unfair world, mate. Only the toughest make it.'

Justin stood in the doorway with a semi-masticated matchstick poking out of the side of his mouth.

'Go on then, Ang, your go.' And he leered over Angus's shoulder during the deliberations that followed. 'Cor, I can see a nifty word there, Ang, old chum. Get ya bout a hundred points.' Eventually Angus took his go. Justin burst out laughing. 'Four points! Four measly bloody points! Is that the best you can do? I dunno why the government wastes so much dough on educating thickoos like you.'

This was the moment when Angus stormed out of the room.

'No sportsmanship, that's the trouble with kids today,' Justin said. Angus mumbled some obscenity from the safety of the stairs. 'Come ere and say that and I'll box yer ears, sunny Jim!' Angus made no reply this time.

'Please, Justin,' I said.

'What's up wiv you then? Poncing round in bed all fuckin day.'

'I've been ill.'

'Yeah, I eard about that. You look all right now though. Honest, you wanna get out of ere, mate. The world's passing ya by.'

'Well, I expect I'll be up any day now.'

'Yeah, right. I tell ya what, I eard about your scholarship lark then.'

'Yes.'

'That's pretty good then, aint it?' He was removing the crushed matchstick from his mouth. 'You get a lot of dough for doin that then?'

'I'll get a grant, it's not very much.'

'Yeah? You wanna get out and make some bread. When d'you start then?'

'October.'

'Shit, right. Be a laugh then, won't it? I tell ya what, I'm setting up in business.'

'I thought you were staying on at school to do A levels.'

'Na, fuck that for a lark. I sold all that old gear out of the lab. That's what give me the idea. I tell ya, it's a cinch makin a bit of cash. Got about sixty quid. Half that's yours, of course.'

'Did you get rid of the mice okay?'

'Not yet, mate. There aint really a market for mice at the moment. I'm gonna wait till I can get a decent price for em. Oh yeah, and I kept your books. I reckoned you'd need them for college and that.'

'Thanks.' The books he spoke of were those in my alternative library, the sort of books it would have worried Ken and Alice to find. The *Shorter History*, the five-volume *Theory and Practice of Necromancy*, *The 120 Days of Sodom* and a number of specialist scientific journals. I was less certain than Justin that I would have any need of these volumes for the continuation of my studies.

'Justin, you didn't sell anything that was recognisable as stolen property?'

'Na! You must reckon I'm a right drongo. We buried all that, right?' He looked about the room for somewhere to deposit his old match, then took out a new one and chewed on that. 'Anyway, all them books is round my new place — I've moved out of Dad's, see.'

'He was serious about that then?'

'Shit, yeah. I don't reckon e's ever gonna say nuffin to me ever again like. E really hates me, I tell ya. I still goes round there. Gets Gail to do me washin and that. When e's at work.'

'That's very nice of Gail to do your washing.'

'Na, she likes it, see. Woman's work.'

'I can't imagine she actively enjoys doing your washing, Justin.'

'Na, that's where you're wrong see, mate. Birds, that's what they like doin. They love it. They make out they don't, gives em summin to blab on about, see.'

'I see.' His world-view continued to hold surprises for me, but I felt little desire to take issue with him. To suggest, for instance, that Gail might do his washing under duress or out of a misguided sense of sympathy. 'Have you seen anything of Norman?'

'Norm? Fuck, yeah. E took Gail out the uver night. I couldn't believe it. I tell ya, some birds are weird, mate. What's she wanna see im for?'

'Perhaps she finds him less demanding than some of the male company she's been subjected to over the years.'

'Well, must be summin like that. E's really serious about er.'

'I hope they make each other happy.'

'Yeah.' He didn't really seem capable of grasping this.

'So tell me, Justin, where have you moved to?'

'Yeah,' he said again, walked over and gazed out of the window. He didn't say anything for a few moments. 'I've moved in wiv Sylvia for a bit.'

'Yes?'

'There's another weird bird, mate.' He turned and nodded grimly. Then shook his head. 'Weird,' he repeated, seeming to relish the consonance of the word.

'Did you sort out all that about the lab and that with her?'

'Oh yeah, that was no problem.' He paused to gouge some wax from his ear. 'I dunno how to tell ya this, mate. I mean, she really is, you know, I mean. She wants to do some really weird things. You know what I'm saying?'

I nodded uncertainly.

'I mean most birds just, you know, just wanna do it normal like, but she aint like that . . . ' and he tailed off into another dumbfounded movement of his head. Some time passed before he spoke again. 'Have you ever been wiv a bird like that?'

'Like what exactly?'

'Well, you know . . . I mean, it's embarrassing to tell ya. Like some of them things in them books of yours.'

'Well, no, I haven't ever done many of those things.'

'Well, that's the kind of thing she's into, mate. I tell ya, it knackers me out for one thing. I haven't got a decent night's sleep all week. I keep avin to get a quick kip in the afternoons.'

'Justin, can you tell me. Did you manage to shut your old man up?'

'Yeah, he aint gonna blab. I told ya I'd sort that out.'

'How did you stop him?'

'It's best I don't tell ya about that, mate. All right?'

He spoke with a simplicity that disguised the sadness in his voice. Everything disguised this sadness: the bravura and the nonchalant chomping on the matchstick. He seemed to be avoiding his own gloom.

'Sorry, I just wondered.'

Again there was silence for a while. Justin had turned back to the window and was watching something in the road. His foot tapped lightly as if to the beat of an imagined song. 'It was summin he did to my mum. Just before she got ill and that.' He stopped, discovered another match in his pocket and put it between his teeth. He cracked it into little segments. 'I was just little, like, and they was avin this argument. He was drunk and that, see, and he pushed er down the stairs. That was when she ad to go into hospital. I never told im I seen that.'

I didn't say anything. He waited a while and then spoke again.

'Anyway, I reckon I'll come up and see ya some time in Cambridge.'

'Oxford.'

'Right. Be a laugh, won't it. You and all them ponces.'

'Mm.'

'Yeah. A right laugh.'
'Tell me about your business then.'
'Aah, it's not much. Just sellin stuff, you know.'
'Who are you selling to?'
'Door-to-door mainly, housewives and that. I tell ya, mate, there's so many bored chicks round ere, you know, husband out at work all day, kids at school. You just knocks on the door, says hello, chat em up a bit and Bob's your arsehole.'
I was laughing at this.
'Na, straight up. I could sell em anything. Get in the door, ave a quick chinwag, give em the eye if they looks like they're a bit randy, and you could sell em a piece a yer shit. You know that old vacuum cleaner we ad when we built that oxygen tent for Norm? Yeah? I got ten quid off this bird for that. No lie. She's really givin me the old come-on, so I says if she's interested in the old vac I'll come back in a week and see it's workin okay. "That's all part of the service," I tells er. So she buys it so I'll go back and see er next week.'
'Will you?'
'Yeah, why not? Cleaner won't work but she don't give a fuck about the cleaner anyway, does she? Probably aint even tried it. She just wants me to knock er up.'
'Will you do that?'
'Might do. Depends. Bit of an old dog but ya don't ave to look at em, do ya? I tell ya though, that Sylvia's really shaggin me out. Fuck me.' He took to shaking his head again.
'And you're going to sell the mice?'
'Yeah. I haven't done that yet. Different market, see. You gotta aim them at the kids, the little ones. Then they goes runnin to their mums and says they wanna mouse. The kid goes on long enough and they buys it a mouse so it'll shut up and they can ave a bit of chinwag wiv me, see. Market research, that is.'
'How much do you charge per mouse?'
'Depend entirely on the buyer, my son. You susses em out, asks for a price, then gives em the old spiel about "I tell ya what, for you, my love, and I'm givin it away at the price . . ." You know what I mean? Presentation, like. Image. Yeah, and about that money I owes ya for the stuff I already sold – '
'I really don't want it.'

'Na! It's yours, mate. But right now I've got it invested in new stock so it's gonna be a week or two, if that's okay wiv you. I could raise it now if you needs it but – '

'Please, really, Justin. You sold the stuff – '

'No way. That thirty quid's yours, and there'll be another ten or so on the mice, and you take twenty per cent on the profit I makes from the investment. Can I say fairer than that?'

I was laughing again.

'Straight up, mate. You won't get nowhere givin it away. That's your money.'

'Well, all right. Whenever it's convenient.'

'Right. You're a mate.' He walked back towards the door now and stopped. 'Look, I hope you get off your arse soon. When ya do, come round to Sylvia's and we'll all ave a booze-up, right? I've gotta skedaddle off now and shift some gear, but you come round and we'll get pissed up. All right?'

'I will, Justin.'

'Yeah, and I'll tell ya one thing, I could do wiv a hand there. You know, if you wanna shack up with Sylvia again you'll be doin me a favour, mate.'

'Well, I might take you up on that.'

'Right. Oh yeah, and that suitcase you took.'

'Sorry I didn't bring it back. I'll try and get it if you want, but it – '

'Na, you miss the point, my son.' He stopped and stood there grinning at me. I suddenly realised that he was suppressing his laughter. 'Na, you see, that's fine. Cos I got another one just like it.'

I did not immediately understand what it was he was saying.

'Yeah, I mean it's identical like.'

'You mean – ?'

He had burst out laughing. 'You didn't reckon I was gonna let my oldest mate do twenty years bird, did ya? I sussed out your game right away.'

'You – you knew about . . . '

'Course I did. You was acting like a nutter. I knew you was gonna do summin stupid.'

'So what happened to the snakes?'

'I took em where we said we'd put em. Down the Porters's. You aint half a nurd.'

'But I – I . . .'

He grinned triumphantly, winked, and disappeared on to the landing.

Appendage

I work in my own laboratory now. I come in at 9.30 and Norman is already here. He's in his lab coat on the other side of a bench covered with petri dishes, setting out my day's work. He grunts to acknowledge my arrival.

He is my lab assistant and looks after the dogs. I got him the job. He was working in the Abbey National and was engaged to a plump little girl called Liz who worked down the road in the bank. They had met at a party and saved up enough money to put down a mortgage on their Barratt home. Saturdays, when Norman could get the day off, they went round the shops together and made a list of the things they'd have in their new home: a Magimix and toaster with Donald Duck on the side, and a special new sort of kettle with a gauge that tells you how much water there is, and an acrylic frog the mouth of which houses a used tea-bag, and a similar hippopotamus that gapes its jaw for a scouring pad. Glass macaw peanut-dispenser, de luxe electric carving knife with optional wall-mounting, true Italian-style ceramics and Summer Breeze tea service.

I couldn't bear to see him doing this to himself. I rang him up at the building society and persuaded him to come and look after the dogs. It was what he had always wanted to do since Mr Burton made us all write down our ambitions. He cleans out their cages and exercises them on the running belt, feeds them and tends to their medical disorders. I sit and watch through the half-open door as he spoons out the cans of Chum and the dogs start baying from the invisible pens behind him, their paws clawing over the steel grids. 'All right!' he says, 'keep your air on. Malcolm! Stop putting your nose through there, you bad boy. You'll get them sores again.' Then the paper rustles as he dips his arm down into the sack of meal and pulls up a beakerful. Ahoooouuw! The dogs bay.

The feeding bowls are arranged in neat, uniform rows along the bench. He stirs the meat and meal together with a long wooden spatula, and the barks of anticipation grow, sharp little yaps, vigorous snuffling noises as the dogs try to eat the air and its fragrant molecules. Norman goes along the rows grinding a Bob Martin's into the bowls of the vitamin-deficient dogs. He talks to the dogs while he does this. 'Becky's avin a Bob Martin's, aint ya?' Becky bays at him. Then he opens each pen and puts a bowl in, and the rattling and barking reach epidemic proportions as the first few dogs bury their snouts.

Then it's tea-time. Karen, my research assistant, drops three tea-bags into the tannin-stained mugs. 'Who wants a bit of Kit-Kat?' she says. 'Sorry it's sticky, I left my bag by the radiator.'

'That must have been it,' I say.

'There's no need to be sarcastic,' she says.

'I wasn't being sarcastic. I'm sorry if I gave that impression. Would you like one of my Mr Kipling Country Slices? They're in my drawer.'

'Shouldn't. I'm supposed to be on a diet.' She giggles. The ritual with the sweets, biscuits and cakes is like this every day. We find the pettiest things to row about and then Karen sulks and refuses to speak when I become abusive. Norman sits throughout in the corner saying very little. Then he shuffles off to prepare a dog for an experiment.

Christmas, Easter and some point in the summer I go home for a few days. At Christmas Alice goes round the new house squirting artificial snow in little artistic patches, shading the windowpanes and arranging dainty cascades down the tree. Angus works in John Menzies now and keeps talking about moving out into his own flat. Last Christmas Christine and her husband came for drinks. Dick, her husband, works for IBM and nods a lot while he talks. They have a baby and she's pregnant again. They live on the new estate a couple of miles away. The same one Norman would have been living on with Liz had I not rescued him.

Norman still talks about Justin. His business career didn't last long so he moved to London and formed a punk band called Refuse Collection. He signed on and wrote songs all day on his out-of-tune Woolworths guitar. Norman acquired a copy of his first single, 'I Torture You', on the independent Dog's Brain label. Since then he has followed Justin's career with meticulous attention. It has progressed through a number of images and degrees of musical sophistication, from the second single, 'Hollywood Glue Sniffin Massacre' (three power chords), through to his most recent synthesiser epic, 'Tibetan Landscape Tones'. Norman loves them all. Sometimes he plays them on his cassette recorder in the lab and the dogs try and sing along. Karen tells him to turn that awful row down. 'That's my mate's band,' he retorts. But we haven't seen him for years.